Quiz inside: Are you changing yourself for your guy?

D1371646

If only I could tell her who I really was . . .

She looked up at me, her eyes shining, then shut them, her dark lashes sweeping down. I didn't shut mine—I was memorizing each of her features.

Then I kissed her very, very gently on her cheek, almost touching her mouth.

"That's it?" she asked after a moment. "That's what I've been waiting for?"

Go for it, whispered a little voice inside me. *Don't be an idiot. She's gorgeous. She's waiting.*

"That's my Christmas kiss?" she exclaimed with disbelief.

But she was waiting for *Quinn,* and when I left Deer Hill, the real Quinn would never show up. She'd be left with a broken heart.

We stared at each other for a long moment. My heart was banging like a sledgehammer. I wondered that she couldn't hear it.

"Okay," she said, standing up. "My mistake. Merry Christmas." She was mad. "May all your secret dreams come true."

Don't miss any of the books in *Love Stories*
—the romantic series from Bantam Books!

Love Stories

Love Happens . . .

Elizabeth Chandler

BANTAM BOOKS
NEW YORK • TORONTO • LONDON • SYDNEY • AUCKLAND

RL 6, age 12 and up

LOVE HAPPENS . . .

A Bantam Book / January 1998

Produced by Daniel Weiss Associates, Inc.
33 West 17th Street
New York, NY 10011.
Cover photography by Michael Segal.

ISBN: 0-553-49217-9

Published simultaneously in the United States and Canada

Bantam Books are published by Bantam Books, a division of Bantam
Doubleday Dell Publishing Group, Inc. Its trademark, consisting of the
words "Bantam Books" and the portrayal of a rooster, is Registered in
U.S. Patent and Trademark Office and in other countries. Marca
Registrada. Bantam Books, 1540 Broadway, New York, New York 10036.

PRINTED IN THE UNITED STATES OF AMERICA

OPM   0 9 8 7 6 5 4 3 2 1

To Cindy, a gutsy woman with a generous heart

One

MY MOTHER WANTED Emily Bellaire's phone number.

"I, uh, can't remember, Mom," I said. The lie traveled over thousands of miles of telephone wire. "And I've already packed it."

"Can't you unpack it?"

"I'll call you," I told her. "Christmas Day, okay? I love you," I added, because I meant it, and because it always puts an end to questions while my mother dabs her eyes. The last thing I needed was Mom calling me at the Bellaires', asking to speak to "Jeff."

Meanwhile, my roommate, Quinn, E-mailed his parents in London, saying he'd phone them on Christmas. In fact, he planned to call them on December 23 and 24 as well, just to make sure they'd have no reason to call him. The last thing *Quinn* needed was his parents calling Emily

Bellaire's house, asking to speak with him—and talking to me.

I guess this sounds confusing. I'd better begin at the beginning.

It was Monday, December 22, minutes away from vacation, minutes away from returning to my room at Maplecrest Preparatory and packing my bags for home. Outside our classroom the big clock bonged, but old Fogarty continued to give out blue books. A few guys stared down at the grades on their final exams, looking dejected, but most gazed out of the lead-paned windows, watching the snow that had begun to fall.

"A disappointment," old Fogarty said, his eyes barely lifting above his glasses to look at me. "A bitter disappointment. But then, I've come to expect that of you."

My heart thumped. I attend Maplecrest, a prestigious boarding school in New York State, on full scholarship, so I have to keep up my grades. And I had studied my brains out for this exam. I looked at the big red 69, then at the name scrawled sloppily on the blue book.

Fogarty moved on. "Excellent, excellent! As always, a pleasure to read your work, young man!" he said, handing the exam to my roommate. I glanced over at the grade on that blue book: 99.

When Mr. Fogarty had passed us, my roommate gave me a lopsided grin. We quickly exchanged exams. "Jeff Danzig scores again," Quinn whispered to me. "Congrats, roomie."

Our teacher wished everyone a fine holiday, then dismissed us. We rushed out the door like a pack of third-graders.

"When will Fogarty get you and me straight?" I asked.

"As soon as everybody else does," Quinn replied, leaping down the steps two at a time. "No time soon—and where does it get me?" He slowed down at the arched doorway, waiting for me to catch up. "Where?"

I shrugged as if I didn't know what Quinn was referring to, as if I had never heard of his brilliant plan that would allow him to go out with six girls simultaneously—two Friday night, two Saturday, and two Sunday afternoon—without ever breaking a date.

You see, Quinn has short blond hair and blue eyes. So do I. He has a long, straight nose and a squarish jaw. So do I. We both stand five feet eleven, though my feet are bigger.

We've been assigned a room together for the last three years. I realized at the beginning that we sort of resembled each other, but people who don't know us well have claimed we are dead ringers. It didn't take my roommate long to figure out the usefulness of this. About a mile away from Maplecrest is an all-girls boarding school. Many of us guys at the Maple spend our weekends looking longingly in that direction; Quinn has covered the distance—several times over. And he is convinced that since his dates are spaced a week apart, I can

3

help him out with his "overcommitments." The girls will never know the difference, he has insisted repeatedly, even offering to pay for my dates as "Quinn." The other guys think I'm crazy not to take him up on it.

"Hey, Eaton!" shouted a guy named Carville, who was also headed toward the dorm. At Maplecrest, the students like to call one another by their last names. Last names tell others what company your dad owns, whose fortune you are going to inherit one day.

"Eaton, did Danzig agree?"

"Not yet," Quinn replied.

"Agree to what?" I asked him.

Quinn grinned at me, then put his hand on my shoulder. Some kind of sell job was coming. "I've solved the problem for both of us," he announced.

"I didn't know we had a problem."

He nodded solemnly. "Christmas vacation."

"What about it?"

Carville fell into step beside us. "Just ask him," he told Quinn impatiently.

"Ask me what?" I said.

"When are you leaving, Jeff?"

"I told you already—the twenty-third, twenty-fourth, or twenty-fifth." I was flying standby from New York to Phoenix, because that's the only way I could afford to go. Quinn, who, like everyone else in our school, is rolling in money, just couldn't understand why Mom, on her barely minimum wage salary, didn't buy me a full-fare ticket home.

"Stay in the East," he said. "Enjoy Christmas the way it was meant to be celebrated—at Deer Hill."

"Deer Hill? Where Emily Bellaire lives? Do you mean you want me to go with you?"

"Actually," Carville said, "he wants you to go instead."

"Instead?" I should have seen it coming. "In your place? As Quinn Eaton? Forget it!" I started to walk away quickly.

"Wait, wait," said Quinn. "You haven't heard what you're missing."

"I've heard, all right. A skinny girl with a million braces who goes to St. Somebody's, writes boring, boring letters, and doesn't have a life. Just the person I want to spend my holiday with."

Carville and Quinn exchanged uneasy glances.

"Yeah, okay, so Emily's not gorgeous," Quinn said. "She has a nice personality."

"You told me she was uptight and didn't have a sense of humor," I reminded him.

Carville made a face at Quinn. His red hair sparkled with snowflakes, making him look like an elf in a store's Christmas display.

"Well, what I really meant was that Emily's kind of serious and smart," Quinn replied smoothly. "Smart just like you."

Carville nodded in agreement. I wondered what he and Quinn hoped to do over the holiday.

"They'll know I'm not you," I said.

"No, they won't," Quinn replied with certainty.

5

"I've been able to avoid Emily for three years. We've written to each other—it keeps our parents happy—but she doesn't even know what my voice sounds like now."

I pushed open a heavy oak door and we tramped across the dorm's foyer, then passed through a smaller, ornately carved entrance. "Too bad you didn't manage to avoid her a little longer," I said as we started up the stairs.

"Couldn't. My parents will be in Europe till December thirtieth. They arranged the visit for me. There's no way out, except . . ."

"Come on, Danzig," Carville pleaded, puffing a little as he climbed the steps. "You get two weeks in a big house with servants, a limo to drive you around, an indoor swimming pool, stables—"

"What do you guys get?" I asked.

"A week of skiing at Killington," Carville replied, "and my parents won't be there."

"Well, I'm sorry I can't help you out," I said. "But it's a crazy idea, and besides, my mother doesn't have anyone except me and I've got old friends to catch up with. We always camp a few days and—"

"Here's what we'll do," Quinn interrupted. "I'm supposed to go from the twenty-third to the second. But let's say we'll leave it open—if you want, we'll think of some excuse for you to leave early. I'll buy you a round-trip ticket to Phoenix, first class. And I'll pay you an extra two hundred. You can take your mother out to a fancy restaurant to make up for missing Christmas dinner."

We reached a landing. "No."

"Three hundred," Quinn offered.

We climbed more steps.

"Four," he said cheerfully. "That's a hundred for each day, a good deal, I'd say."

I started getting angry. I'd known even before I arrived at Maplecrest that the guys here would be able to buy things I've never dreamed of. That's okay. It's the way they buy favors, the way they buy people, that gets to me.

"I won't do it, Quinn. I've got better things to do than pretend I'm you and spend Christmas with a weird girl."

"Okay," he said, pulling out a key to our dorm room. "I understand. You need some more time to think about it."

"I've thought about it," I almost shouted, "and I'm telling you, nothing, *nothing* will get me to change my mind."

"What do you mean, Christmas is going to be different this year?" I asked as I leaned out the dorm window, clutching Quinn's cordless. I watched a snowball battle on the quad below.

A long sigh and some static traveled the phone line from Arizona to New York. "I'm really sorry, Jeff," my mother said. "But you know Aunt Bet took me in when I was a young girl with nowhere else to go. She needs me now. I really have to go

7

to Seattle. I, uh, I've called your father."

"You what?"

"It would be no fun for you at Aunt Bet's," she reasoned. "She has a studio apartment and full-time nurses, as well as other people coming in and out. Your father was real good about having you come. He said the more the merrier."

Which pretty well describes my father's philosophy, being on his fourth marriage and having had children with all four wives. I visited him one Christmas at his third wife's home in a Mexican border town. It was like attending a convention, especially with the name tags worn by all of us half- and stepsiblings.

There was a long silence.

"Jeff? Jeff, are you there? Try to understand—"

"I understand," I said. "Really, I do, Mom. Maybe it would be best if I stayed here."

"But isn't the dormitory closed?" she asked. "Where would you go?"

Where could I go? "Well, I sort of have an invitation."

"You do? A friend?" she asked.

"A friend of Quinn's." Cripe! What was I saying?

"Oh, honey, that's wonderful!" she replied, sounding relieved.

"Of course, now that I think about it, Dad might be hurt—"

"No, no," she assured me. "I'll explain to him. Don't think twice about it, Jeff."

If only I had.

*   *   *

8

The long black limo pulled up to the curb and a uniformed man got out. "I'm Robert Dove," the driver said politely. "Call me Robert."

"Nice to meet you," I mumbled. I could never call a man my father's age "Robert."

The chauffeur looked at me strangely when I tried to load my pile of luggage into the trunk. He hurried around to the car door and held it open for me, as if he were eager to stuff me in there and get me out of the way. Then he reached in after me and opened a cabinet, revealing a television, VCR, and CD player, with a collection of tapes and disks. "Perhaps there is something here you will enjoy, sir," he said.

I nodded silently. I think I was numb—Quinn and Carville had kept me up all night, prepping me.

Apparently my three years at Maplecrest haven't taught me much. I'd had no idea that my polyester and rayon blends could be spotted a football field away. I knew nothing about the advantages of merino wool. Quinn and Carville had quickly tutored me on cashmere, and silk ties, and well-cut shirts . . . of course, I'd already forgotten most of it.

I'd worked harder at memorizing family trees and the names of important friends of the Bellaires and Eatons. After drilling me twice on them, Quinn had moved on to reviewing pictures of his trips to Europe. And Greece. And Egypt. Lucky for me that my roommate remembered more about the girls and restaurants than the fine points of history and art. I'd taken notes on the food; my own reading would allow me to bull my way through history and art as well as Quinn ever could.

"What more should I know about Emily?" I'd asked.

Quinn hadn't answered right away, probably deciding what he could say honestly without having me back out.

"Her parents keep a pretty close eye on her. She goes to a really strict school run by nuns."

"So watch your step," Carville had said, snickering.

"Just don't do anything shocking," Quinn had advised.

"Like kiss her hand." Carville couldn't help himself.

"I don't plan to touch her," I'd assured them.

Now the suitcases in the trunk were packed with Quinn's clothes and Carville's shoes. When Quinn wasn't looking, I had sneaked in a comfy old T-shirt and shorts and a favorite photograph. Quinn had said that Deer Hill had ponds, so I took my own ice skates with me. Two shopping bags full of gifts, which had been purchased by Quinn and wrapped up in silver and gold by Saks, were also packed. One of Quinn's credit cards, a phone card, and a wad of cash were now stuffed in my wallet. It felt lumpy in my pocket.

"Pardon me, Mr. Eaton, do you need any assistance in operating the entertainment equipment?"

For a moment I didn't realize the polite question from the front seat was directed at me.

"No—no, thanks very much. I think I can figure it out."

But I didn't. We had barely cleared school property when my eyes shut. An hour later, according to Quinn's Rolex, I opened them and glanced around at the hills and woods and low stone walls of the Connecticut countryside.

Mr. Dove smiled a little into the rearview mirror. I wiped the damp corner of my mouth, hoping I hadn't been sleeping with my mouth wide open and drooling.

"A refreshing nap, sir?"

What was the proper answer? "Why yes, Robert, delightful"? But the words wouldn't come out. I simply nodded.

I was wide awake now, wondering how seriously boring and prim Emily Bellaire was. As for brains, she had to be a lot smarter than a guy who'd get himself involved in such a ridiculous scheme.

Two

THE TALL GATES of Deer Hill swung inward. We passed a little steep-roofed house, then cruised a driveway with trees along each side. I saw the chimneys of the house first, and a few minutes later the house itself, a huge gray stone structure, three stories tall. It reminded me of a place I had seen in a British movie, with its left and right arms—wings, I guess you call them—creating a rectangular court-yard in front of it.

Mr. Dove let me out of the car and we climbed the front steps together, entering a hall as big as the entire bungalow Mom and I rent in Arizona. The ceilings were incredibly high; you could have set up basketball hoops without worrying about the crystal chandelier. To the left, a curved staircase swept up to a second-floor balcony.

I was led to the back of the large hall and left in a room Mr. Dove called the library. "Mr. Bellaire is in the city, occupied with business," he informed me. "Mrs. Bellaire will be seeing you shortly for tea. Miss Emily as well, of course."

"Of course."

As soon as he disappeared I wanted to rush after him and beg him to take me to LaGuardia Airport. I was trying to figure out whether I could bribe him with the cash Quinn had given me when I heard a low, ugly growl. In the movies, estates like these always have swift and powerful dogs, Dobermans that track you down the moment you make a break for the road. I turned around, but where the head of the vicious animal should have been was simply a brass doorknob. Three feet lower stood a hairy little thing with green and red bows tied to its head.

Hardly a Doberman. Still, it bared sharp little teeth that I preferred not to have sunk into my leg. "Nice doggy."

Its hairy lip quivered. It inched toward me. I inched toward the door that led back to the entrance hall.

"Hey, little buddy," I said softly.

Maybe it didn't like being little. The next moment its jaws were clamped firmly to my pants—I mean, Quinn's pants. "Hey, want to play, pal?" I asked optimistically as it tugged at the fine merino wool. Then I felt the dog's hard nose jammed against my calf. Its growl deepened and I knew it was going to bite. I quickly lifted my leg and swung it forward.

The dog flew across the polished floor, sliding like a mop that had lost its handle. Then it was up on its feet again, making more ugly noises. This time it didn't inch. It lunged. But I was one step ahead, already in the hall, pulling the door closed behind me. Desperate scratching came from the other side of the door. Then I heard peals of laughter from above me.

I thought they were laughing at me, but I couldn't see anyone. As I stepped out from the shadow of the overhead balcony, I spotted two girls, one with shoulder-length reddish brown curls and another with silky black hair that fell slightly past her chin.

"How much do you want to bet, Lon?" the dark-haired girl asked, waving around a big dust rag.

"I know you too well to make a bet," the other replied.

Then the black-haired girl turned to look down the long sweep of stairway. I should have made sure I was out of sight, but I just stood there and stared.

It had never occurred to me that some of the employees of the house might be my age. It hadn't crossed my mind that one of them might be beautiful. Did maids live on the estate? Maybe in that little house by the gates, I thought. Things were looking brighter!

The dark-haired girl placed the dust cloth on the stairway's wide bannister. I blinked—in one quick movement, she was up and sitting on it sidesaddle. With the cry of a wild bird, she came sailing down the long curved railing, her arms out for balance and her hair streaming behind her. She picked up speed near the bottom and flew off the end like a kid jumping from a swing. *Thump!*

I took two quick steps back into the shadows.

The girl stood up slowly, smiling to herself, rubbing her back end, then turned to grin at Lon. She pumped her fist once in the air.

But the girl at the top of the steps had turned away to look over her shoulder.

"Miss Emily, Miss Emily," someone called from upstairs.

"It's Gamby!" Lon hissed. Each of the maids ran a different way, leaving me alone in the hall.

Alone, that is, until Gamby came down the stairs.

"I am Miss Gambrini, the housekeeper," the gray-haired lady told me, then escorted me back into the library. As soon as the little dog saw Gamby, it skulked beneath a long table, then ran toward the door through which it had first come. I breathed a sigh of relief. Five minutes later Mr. Dove brought me to the drawing room.

"Quinn," said Mrs. Bellaire, rising from her chair, holding out her hand.

I tried to exude Quinn's natural confidence and

reached to shake her hand firmly, but her fingers fled through mine like icy little fish.

Next to a large fireplace stood a table with a silver pot and a set of small china cups. Quinn had told me that Mrs. Bellaire was British and to expect teatime around four o'clock. "Do sit down," Mrs. Bellaire said, gesturing to a chair that was covered with some shiny flowered material. There were flowers on all the chairs, flowers on all the curtains, flowers on the rugs. I looked for skinny Emily in a matching flowered dress.

"You've changed," Mrs. Bellaire said, studying me.

"Really?" My voice cracked a little.

"You don't look as much like your father anymore."

"Really?"

"I see more of your mother in you now."

"Oh."

"Of course," she continued, "our Emily has grown up quite a bit as well. And she has been so looking forward to your stay with us."

"Really?"

"Really," someone mocked. She was standing in the hall doorway. "The truth is, I didn't know that you were coming till this morning."

I rose quickly—as Quinn had told me to do—then caught my breath. It was the maid with the black hair.

"Emily, dear, do let us see your more gracious side," her mother said.

16

I stared at Emily in disbelief. What lousy luck! Where was the skinny, weird girl from the convent school who had a mouthful of braces?

Emily crossed the room. I tried to shake her hand as delicately as her mother had shaken mine. She crunched my fingers—on purpose, I was pretty sure—then sat down by her mother like a little princess.

"Of course, since the moment I was told you were visiting," Emily said, "I've just been in a flurry of excitement getting ready."

"The bannister sure looks good," I remarked.

She turned sharply, her green eyes betraying her surprise.

"Pardon me?" Mrs. Bellaire inquired.

"Tea, Mum," Emily said quickly. "Please? I'm wilting."

While Mrs. Bellaire turned her attention to pouring tea, Emily looked me up and down with new interest. I returned her gaze and she laughed silently. She was gorgeous. Obviously she and Quinn hadn't been exchanging photos along with their letters.

I was handed a teacup, green-and-gold-painted china that was thin as paper. I could not keep it from rattling in its saucer. Determined not to let beautiful Emily think she could make me nervous, I curled my finger through the cup's twiglike handle to steady it. When I tried to lift the tea to my mouth, I realized my mistake. It couldn't be done, not at that angle, not without having my elbow

17

sticking out like a disjointed turkey wing. But my finger was stuck. I couldn't move my big, stupid finger in or out of the thin loop of the handle. Every time I tried, tea sloshed over the side.

Mrs. Bellaire chatted away about a fundraiser and all the money they were going to raise for poor people who had such miserable Christmases. Emily said, "Yes . . . yes . . . yes, Mum," while daintily sipping from her cup and watching me. The corners of Emily's pretty mouth kept curling up.

I knew I'd have to snap off the handle or walk around for the next ten days with a teacup stuck on my finger. Just when I thought things couldn't get worse, I heard a *jingle-jingle* in the hall.

"Hello, little Pansy," Mrs. Bellaire called.

The mop dog came trotting in, then stopped, focusing its beady little eyes on me. It delivered a long and vicious snarl.

"Good heavens!" said Mrs. Bellaire.

"Pansy!" Emily chastised the dog.

The dog growled. I figured this time Pansy would go for the jugular. If I couldn't get the teacup off my finger, it'd be a messy scene.

"What has gotten into you, Pansy-Pan?" Mrs. Bellaire said to the hairy mop. "Three years ago, you adored Quinn."

Pansy's growl deepened, proving that dogs aren't as easy to fool as people.

"I'd better put her in another room, Mum," Emily said, scooping up the dog.

18

But before she got any farther, we heard a commotion out in the hall. Loud voices. A door slammed, then another. Something metallic fell on the hard marble floor and sent rolling echoes throughout the house.

"Sounds like Harper's home," Emily observed dryly.

I thought back to the previous night's cram session and what Quinn had told me about Harper Bellaire: Emily's older brother, big, klutzy, attends Harvard.

There was a heavy thud.

"Ow!" someone exclaimed. He sounded very unhappy.

"Sorry. Sorry," another male voice apologized.

Mrs. Bellaire rose swiftly and moved two empty chairs so they were farther away from the fragile tea table. While her back was turned, I raised my arm in its wing position and gulped down the hot tea. Mrs. Bellaire picked up a delicate vase and moved it to a higher, safer spot on the fireplace mantel. Meanwhile I worked like crazy to get the empty cup off my finger. Emily, who was carrying the dog to the door, glanced over her shoulder. Her face didn't reveal what she had seen.

"Robert, would you take Pansy, please?" she asked.

Then, like stage actors, we all fell back into our proper positions as a guy about my age entered.

"You must be Harper's friend," Mrs. Bellaire said graciously.

"Yes, ma'am. Dixon Tully," he replied, coming forward.

His face reminded me of a soap opera star's. His hair was thick and brown and perfectly styled. He was the same height as I, though a little slimmer. He looked around the room in a smooth, confident way. Most girls would probably find him attractive, I thought. Emily was sure taking in the details.

"Dixon Tully the third, isn't it?" Mrs. Bellaire inquired. "It's a pleasure to have Senator Tully's son, Governor Tully's grandson, with us. . . . Emily, dear? This is my daughter."

Emily reached out. I saw the look of surprise on Dixon's face and knew she had crunched his fingers too.

"And our longtime family friend, Quinn Eaton."

Dixon shook my hand without meeting my eyes, but examined my clothes as if he were planning to buy them.

"Please sit down," Mrs. Bellaire said, "and tell us all if Harvard is treating you well."

Dixon took my seat, between Emily and her mother.

"Well enough, but I'm glad the semester is over," he replied, smiling. I detected a trace of a southern accent. "And I'd rather hear all about Deer Hill."

Mrs. Bellaire glowed. "Do you like what you've

seen so far?—Ah, here you are, Harper," she said, looking up, sounding at once happy and distressed to see her son.

He was a huge guy, not fat, but broad all over, with dark bristly hair and brown eyes. If he was trying to look macho by not shaving for a day or two, he had failed. Quinn's description of Harper three years ago was still accurate: a large teddy bear.

Harper hugged Emily, then kissed his mother carefully on the cheek.

"You're scratchy," Mrs. Bellaire complained.

He turned to me, smiling. "So you made it, Quinn." He sat down. "Let's eat."

Mrs. Bellaire sighed.

Harper's request was soon answered. The girl with reddish hair I had seen at the top of the stairway walked into the room carrying a tray with all kinds of little cookies and fancy cakes. "My mom asked me to bring these in," she explained.

"Hey, Lonnie," Harper said softly, "you're home." He stood up. So did I, though I noticed that Dixon remained seated.

Mrs. Bellaire turned to Lonnie. "Thank you, dear. Lonnie, these are our guests, Dixon Tully the third and Quinn Eaton."

Lonnie smiled. "Pleased to meet you."

"Lonnie's parents are two of our best employees," Mrs. Bellaire explained. "Lonnie's home from college for Christmas break."

Lonnie looked uncomfortable, and I felt rather

embarrassed myself. Mrs. Bellaire's introduction was so patronizing. "Nice to meet you," I said to Lonnie. Dix didn't say anything.

Lonnie was definitely used to Harper. The next moment, he lurched forward and knocked into her and the tray. She quickly stepped aside and, with an impressive recovery of balance, safely delivered the tea cakes to their table.

I sat down, but Harper remained standing, his big arms dangling, looking like a bear that had just lumbered into a picnic grove. He hugged Lonnie, as he had his sister, and she hugged him back, but they both looked awkward.

Harper stepped back. "Looking good," he said in a tone that could have been meant for another guy. I half expected to see him punch her in the arm.

"Thanks. You too."

"So, how do you like Maryland?" he asked.

"Love it," she replied.

"Do you? Wonderful."

"The courses I'm taking are really interesting. And the social life's great," she added.

"Glad to hear it," Harper said stiffly.

"Lonnie's found a terrific apartment near campus," Emily interjected, her voice rising over her mother's, who had started telling Dixon about the fund-raiser for miserable people at Christmas.

"I thought you were in a freshman dorm," Harper recalled, frowning.

"Well, I've made a lot of friends," Lonnie answered with a smile. "The whole house is Maryland students."

"Guys too?" he asked.

"Sure."

"Lonnie, dear," Mrs. Bellaire said, her voice arching over everyone else's, "do sit down. After all, you really are almost part of the family."

Lonnie had pale Irish skin and gray-blue eyes. Now she blushed and looked even prettier than before. "Thank you, but I promised my mother I'd help her in the kitchen," she said, and made a quick exit.

"Sit down, Harper," Mrs. Bellaire ordered. "You were saying, Dixon . . . ?"

"Well, simply that I would enjoy working at the Carriage House Sale with you and Emily. Surely I could be of some help this evening, with all those ladies descending like vultures on the designer clothes."

Harper glanced at Dixon and screwed up his face. It did seem weird, as if Dixon was flirting with Mrs. Bellaire, but I knew what was going on—he was trying to score some brownie points before he pursued Emily.

Emily glanced at me. "Would you also like to come?"

"Not really," I replied, and Harper snorted. *Not if your mother and Dixon are going with us,* I thought. *Why should I spend an evening with lots of fussy old women picking over clothes?* Quinn

23

Eaton didn't plan to chase Emily. And Jeff Danzig, being just Jeff Danzig, couldn't. Given my circumstances, I knew it could be dangerous to spend too much time with her.

"Dinner is served promptly at seven, Quinn," Mrs. Bellaire said. "Harper will show you and Dixon your rooms in the east wing. Your luggage is already there. Dixon, the car will be brought around at five-thirty. Cook will pack us something to eat, since we won't be returning till eleven."

I put my teacup and cake plate on the tray. Then I took Harper's from him, stacking the dishes neatly. Emily glanced sideways at me. I remembered too late that proper houseguests in places like this didn't do anything but be served.

It was a relief, ten minutes later, when Harper deposited Dixon and me in the east wing. Harper apologized for the fact that he wouldn't be joining me for dinner and said he hoped I didn't mind entertaining myself for the evening.

A pool table, Ping-Pong table, large-screen TV, VCR, and two computers with games occupied the floor below the guest rooms. "I think I can find something to do," I told him.

Alone in my room, I went immediately to the window. The wing across the courtyard was illuminated with soft white lights—the main house too shimmered in the twilight. Someone was standing in the darkening courtyard, gazing up at the house. After a moment I realized it was Emily, her arms

24

folded around her as if she were cold. I lit my window candles to make the glittering winter scene perfect for her. She turned as if she had noticed and I stepped back quickly.

During Christmas at home, Mom puts a different-colored bulb in each window. I string red lights shaped like chili peppers around the front door. Our lights blink rather than twinkle. Now *that's* perfect.

Three

"SOUP, SIR?" MR. Dove asked.
"Thanks."

He served me, then left me alone in the dining room to slurp and stare down the long polished table. Four NBA players lined up head to foot could have slept on it. I wondered if Emily had ever taken off her shoes and slalomed down the table, weaving in and out around the gleaming silver candleholders.

Quinn's view of Emily puzzled me. I guess a person could change a lot in three years, but I had the feeling that Emily had been riding bannisters since she was four. Maybe Quinn had only seen the side of her that the Bellaires wanted him to see.

Mr. Dove brought in salmon, which was served with lots of tiny little vegetables. Rich people are strange. They have big gates, big fireplaces, and big chandeliers like the two that were glittering above me, but teeny little teacups, little baby vegetables, and small, vicious dogs.

I knew I was eating good stuff, but I longed for my mother's fat french fries and tree limbs of broccoli. Sighing, I gathered up the plates with my unfinished dinner and the battery of silverware and carried them to the door through which Mr. Dove kept disappearing. I followed the sound of voices, passing through what looked like a breakfast room. As soon as I entered the kitchen, the friendly chatter stopped. It was as if I were a restaurant customer who had suddenly barged into forbidden territory.

Mr. Dove got up quickly from a table against the wall. "Is something wrong, sir?"

Gambrini wiped her mouth. Her big feet searched under the table for her shoes. The man next to her lowered his fork and looked at me curiously. Over by the sink stood a round woman with a nice face—Lonnie's Irish face. She wiped her hands on an apron and peered around the big hulk of Harper to see what I was carrying. That was the weirdest thing of all: Harper was sitting at a work table in the middle of the kitchen, chowing down.

"Everything was great, but I'm done now," I explained, carrying the dishes over to the sink.

The round lady, who must have been Mrs. Dove, studied my half-filled plate. I glanced back at Harper's. He was scarfing down scrambled eggs, home fries, and jelly toast. I wanted his dinner.

"Pull up a seat," Harper said, his mouth full.

The adults exchanged looks.

"Didn't eat too much," he observed, pointing at my plate with his fork.

"Dessert, sir?" Mr. Dove asked, taking my dishes from me.

I saw some kind of little multicolored thing sitting on a fancy piece of china. "No, thanks."

Mrs. Dove continually rubbed her hands on her apron. When I sat down on a stool next to Harper's, she set a glass in front of me the same size as his and filled it with milk. Then she gave me a plain blue plate and opened two tins, one filled with brownies, the other with homemade chocolate chip cookies. Harper reached out and she slapped his fingers lightly.

"Not till you've finished your dinner. I opened them for Mr. Quinn."

"Oh, Dovey, come on."

She shook her head.

"Just one? One little itsy-bitsy—"

"Don't whine. I raised you better than that." Her voice was crisp, but she was smiling at him. I didn't feel homesick anymore, and helped myself to both brownies and cookies.

Gamby and the other man picked up their conversation, and Mr. Dove, shrugging, joined them again.

"Mr. Quinn, let me show you where I hide the treats," said Mrs. Dove.

"Dovey!"

The man next to Gamby laughed at Harper, and I turned around.

"Do you know Tony?" Mrs. Dove asked. "Tony Gambrini. Runs the stable and takes care of the grounds."

He waved at me.

"You can't give away my secret stash," Harper pleaded with Mrs. Dove.

She rolled her eyes. "I make enough to feed an army, at least when *you're* home. Now, in this refrigerator, Mr. Quinn, I keep the food prepared according to madam's schedule, so don't touch. But in this one, and in these cupboards on either side, you can have whatever you want."

"Great! Thanks," I said.

Harper grunted, but it was a friendly kind of grunt.

"There's a night-light by the door, and it's always on. The main switch is right above it—just in case you're hungry later on."

"Thanks again!"

I liked the big, warm kitchen with its checked curtains, plain wood cabinets, and coppery shine of pots and pans hanging above the work table. I wished I could eat there every night. Maybe Harper did too.

"You follow sports?" he asked me, picking up a cookie as soon as Mrs. Dove turned her back.

"I'm a Suns fan."

"Yeah? Phoenix?" he said, using the cookie like

a piece of toast to scoop up his last bit of egg.

"The Knicks too," I added quickly, remembering I was supposed to be from the East Coast.

He nodded. "I watch hockey."

"Really? I play it at school," I told him. After years of street hockey in Arizona, I had learned to play it on ice and was pretty good at it.

"Maybe the ponds will freeze over. I'm kind of clumsy, though," Harper admitted quietly.

"Can't be good at every sport."

"Wouldn't mind being good at one," he replied. "Dix will take you on. Dix can take anybody on."

I thought of Dixon at the fund-raiser, cheerfully carrying some lady's pile of packages, scoring points with Emily and her mother. I could really enjoy beating him.

"Have you guys been friends for a long time?" I asked.

"Not really. Dix likes to play tennis and I've got a membership at an off-campus club. It's hard to get a court on campus, you know. Dix likes to play. He gives me a lot of tips— Hey, Lon."

Lonnie had just come in from the outside, walking my favorite little dog. Bits of snow sparkled in Lonnie's hair, and her eyes were bright from the cold. She let the dog drink from a bowl, then quickly picked her up.

"Pansy wouldn't hurt you," she told me, "but I heard she's not a big fan of yours."

"She used to be," Harper observed.

Lonnie scratched the dog and fluffed up her

fur. "I'm going to put her in the library."

When Lonnie returned, she pulled up a stool next to Harper.

"So Mom made some cookies for you, Quinn." She smiled at me.

"They were for *me*," Harper told her, sounding a little hurt.

She threw back her head and laughed. Harper's cheeks turned pink.

"Mom really missed cooking for you, Harp," Lonnie assured him. "She told me so in her letters."

"Did you miss being around here?" he asked. "It was strange, wasn't it, not being home even on the weekends?"

"Yeah, I guess. But remember, I went to high school around here—I was *always* here. Maybe I was gladder than you to get away."

"How come you didn't come home for Thanksgiving?" he asked.

"Just didn't." She shrugged. "Had stuff to do."

"Emily missed you," he said.

Lonnie met his eyes for a moment. I wondered whether Harper was the one who had missed her the most. I was pretty sure he'd never admit it.

"Everybody who stayed at school got together," Lonnie told us. "We cooked a turkey and made stuffing and a pumpkin pie. I made the pie."

"Good," Harper said unenthusiastically.

"What did you do for Thanksgiving?" she asked me.

"Went over to my teacher's house."

31

"Your teacher's house?"

"Why?" Harper asked, surprised.

Cripe. The kitchen was so comfortable, I had forgotten who I was—who I was supposed to be. What had Quinn done for Thanksgiving? Duck hunting.

"Well, my teacher has a farm where people hunt and stuff. And my parents were getting ready to leave for Europe. So . . ." I let the sentence drift off.

"It must be hard not to spend Thanksgiving or Christmas with your family," Lonnie said gently.

This was the first Christmas I would be away from home. I nodded silently.

Harper reached for the largest brownie in the tin and put it on my plate. Comfort food, I guess. He not only looked like a teddy bear, he thought like one.

"So who are some of the people who live in your house?" Harper asked Lonnie.

"Well, there's Gretchen, and Kelly, and Julie, and me. Julie and I room together. Then there's Tom, Mike, Fitz, and Randy. Here, I've got a picture."

She picked up an envelope of photos that had been left on the table and pulled out one that showed eight guys and girls sitting on the steps of an old wooden house. She started naming people as she pointed to them, and didn't see that another photo had slipped out of the envelope. But Harper saw it.

"Who's this?" he asked.

"Uh, Tom."

It was Tom and Lonnie, standing on a porch, their arms loosely around each other. Lonnie was smiling at the camera. Tom was smiling at her.

"You dating him?"

"He's a friend," she said.

"You like him?" Harper persisted.

"I like all my friends," she replied evasively.

"Tom looks like a nice guy," I told her.

"He looks like he likes you," Harper observed, handing her the photo.

"Well," Lonnie said, "I've got some gift wrapping to do, and I better get it done tonight. Mom, Dad," she called to them, "I'm going over."

Mrs. Dove was closing the dishwasher. Gamby, Tony, and Mr. Dove stood up. "Long day tomorrow," Tony said as he and Gamby pulled on coats.

"When you're done," Mrs. Dove said to Harper and me, "just rinse your dishes and leave them in the sink."

"Thanks—thanks very much," I replied.

Harper was in another world.

When everyone had left, I said to him, "I think I'll take a couple of cookies back with me."

"Huh? Oh, sure. Sorry. Too many late nights studying for exams."

"Know how you feel," I replied.

"There's a fridge in the lounge below your room. Take something to drink if you want."

I poured another glass of milk.

"You don't have any trouble with girls, do you," Harper suddenly blurted out.

I started to laugh, then I remembered I was Quinn. "I guess I find dating pretty easy."

"So you always get who you want?"

The truth was that during the school year, I didn't allow myself to want anybody. All the girls I knew through Maplecrest were out of my league. After several had made it clear they weren't interested in someone with no bucks, I gave up.

But as Quinn Eaton, I answered coolly, "Yeah, usually."

"So does Dix," Harper said.

And I bet he tells you all the details, I thought, *maybe some details that never really occurred.* I had heard it all before at Maplecrest.

"Dix sure scored some points with Mum today," Harper added.

"That's okay. I don't want to date your mum."

Harper laughed.

"I think he scored some points with Emily too," he said, still grinning, "though it's hard to tell with her. Em fakes really well. She's nothing like Mum thinks—I guess you figured that out a long time ago."

More like a few hours ago, I thought.

"It'll be fun watching you and Dix. I was sure Dix would like her. And there's nothing he likes better than competition." Harper carried his dishes to the sink. "There's just one thing," he said, then hesitated.

34

"What?"

"This sounds really stupid." He ran his big hand over his mouth. "If you tell her I said this, I'll never hear the end of it."

"So I won't tell her."

"If something gets going between you and Em, don't hurt her," he said quickly. "I know from friends back at Maplecrest you've got a way with girls, and it's none of my business, that's what Emily would say, but just don't, like, hurt her."

He was a teddy bear all the way through.

"I won't. Promise." It seemed like an easy enough vow for Jeff Danzig to keep.

That night I watched *Invasion of the Body Snatchers*. Clone movies are great entertainment, until you find yourself actually parading around as somebody else. I turned it off three quarters of the way through and headed up to my room.

When I opened my suitcase I discovered that someone had carefully hung up the clothes I had brought—including my favorite pair of holey shorts and tattered T-shirt. Luckily, I had hidden the one picture I kept with me inside a paperback. I flipped through the pages. It was still there—my mother, dressed in what I call her "rodeo queen outfit," my old teacher Mrs. Quantos, and me, all of us grinning at the camera, the scholarship letter from Maplecrest in my hands. I had brought my driver's license but had slipped it under Quinn's phone card in Quinn's wallet. That lay on the bureau, apparently undisturbed.

I took a shower and turned on the TV, which I found hidden inside a fancy-looking cupboard. Whoever had decorated the room liked stripes—I felt like I was in a birdcage. The bed was large. It had this dome thing over the pillow end, with curtains coming down from it, something like a roof over a throne. If it fell, I'd be crushed to death.

Even so, with a Christmas special fa-la-laing in the background, and my horror paperback cracked open and my old shorts and shirt on, I felt like me again. I didn't respond to the little knock on the door a few minutes later—I thought it came from the TV. But the knock came again, more sharply this time, and when I looked up at the TV, I saw an advertisement for nasal decongestant.

I got up quickly and opened the bedroom door, expecting Harper or Mr. Dove, or even Quinn back from brownnosing.

"Hello."

"Emily!"

I tried to narrow the opening, but she pushed the door in. Her eyes swept down me, not missing a thing, the shirt like Swiss cheese and the shorts with edges turning into fringe. My eyes didn't miss a thing either, like the slit in her skirt.

For a moment neither of us said anything.

"Emily, why are you here?"

"I live here," she reminded me. "I just came by to see if you had everything you needed." She walked right into the room. I reached back quickly for Quinn's bathrobe. Instead, I snatched up one of those crocheted things people throw over chairs. One side of Emily's mouth moved a little, but she didn't laugh.

Her eyes followed me as I walked to the other side of the room to fetch Quinn's robe off the bed. "I've got everything."

"How do you know?" she asked, then laughed.

Was I supposed to invite her to sit down?

She sat down before I could decide.

"Where's Dix?" I asked. I knew his room was next to mine.

"Getting a snack in the kitchen," she said. "Who's this?"

She had my photograph. I tried to pull it away from her, which had the unintended effect of pulling her closer to me. I smelled her perfume.

"Uh, that's me and two of my teachers."

"Really? Look at the outfit on that one. All she needs is a lasso."

I bit my tongue.

"Her face is nice, though. Truly nice. She looks like a person you can talk to."

"She is," I agreed.

"What school was this?" Emily asked.

She'd know that the rodeo queen and Hispanic

lady couldn't have taught at Maplecrest.

"Elmwood Downs," I said. "It's a very small middle school." Actually, it was the name of a race-track in the paperback I had just been reading, the scene of several bizarre murders.

"You never mentioned it in any of your letters," Emily said.

When I'd asked Quinn to tell me what he had written to her, all he'd said was "stuff." When I'd pressed him, he'd said, "It was too stupid to remember. Stuff."

"By the time we began writing each other, I was in Maplecrest," I pointed out to Emily.

"You know, I showed all your early letters to my friends at school."

I looked at her, surprised. Maybe the letters meant more to her than they did to Quinn. Maybe Harper knew that, which explained his concern that I'd hurt her.

"I wanted everyone to see how romantic they were."

"Romantic?" I said. "Really," I added in a lower, offhand tone that Quinn might use.

"Well, what would *you* call them?" she asked.

I glanced around the room, searching for the right word. "Friendly?"

"Well, maybe the very first one," she replied, moving closer, resting her head of silky black hair against my arm.

I knew that Quinn could talk his way through anything. Had he sweet-talked Emily in his letters, then sweet-talked me into believing he had never said a romantic word to her?

"Don't worry," she said, smiling up at me. "After your letters became . . . passionate"—she said it softly, shyly—"I kept them to myself."

She put her arms around my neck and raised her face to mine.

I stared at her, at her long dark lashes and the curve of her cheek. What was I supposed to do? It was just like Quinn to practice his lines on her, tell her she was everything he ever wanted, then leave me to deal with it.

Not that I couldn't think of an easy way to deal with it—I wanted to kiss Emily Bellaire! She was beautiful. And while I couldn't stand her proper, snotty side, I was intrigued by the side of her not everyone knew about.

But it seemed wrong. Emily wanted Quinn, not me. I'd give her polite little kisses, nothing more.

Her lips moved closer and closer to mine.

"I think I hear Dixon," I said.

It was an obvious and klutzy excuse.

Emily frowned, then pulled away. "What is *wrong* with you?"

Good question, I thought. I had to be crazy not to go for it.

"I dunno," I muttered. "I'm not feeling too much like myself."

"You're tired," she said gently.

"I guess so. I'm really sorry." *Sorry for Quinn's*

stupid games, for my stupid charade, for not play-ing straight with you, I added silently.

"It's okay," she told me, standing up. Then she reached and pulled one of the holes in my T-shirt. "I'll make sure we have plenty of time alone this week."

Four

THE NEXT MORNING Dix and I were given a tour of Deer Hill. It was Christmas Eve and the place was swarming with part-time workers, polishing and decorating for the next day's open house. I found out that Gamby and Tony were sister and brother. Both full-time employees, they occupied the little house close to the entrance gates. Lonnie's parents, also full-time, lived with her in the west wing, the part of the house that was directly across the courtyard from where Dix and I were staying. To get to the main house, the Doves went through an elbow-shaped hallway of windows and skylights that served as a greenhouse.

Emily gave the tour and Harper tagged behind. I didn't know how to act after Emily's late-night visit and at first avoided direct eye contact. But I had no reason to worry. Emily had changed back into the cool-toned, prim and proper daughter. Now I

41

knew where they got these ideas for bewitched-princess tales.

The upstairs of the main house had the family's bedrooms, two smaller guest rooms, several bathrooms, and a music room. Emily's room looked like the rest of the house—covered with flowers and stripes, everything perfectly kept.

"What's your room at school look like?" I asked.

"A room," she said coolly. "Why?"

"Just curious. Rooms tell you about the people who live in them."

She walked on without reply. Emily the ice princess. Maybe this was all Quinn knew about her, and he really hadn't tried to mislead me.

After we finished the house tour, we grabbed our coats and went outside to see the stables. Then we went to see the pool, which was housed with an exercise gym in another building.

Apparently Dix's family had the same taste and shopped the same places the Bellaires did, for so far, according to Dix, everything the Bellaires had, the Tullys had too.

We gathered around the pool to look at a statue of a little boy peeing into it. "It's wonderful!" Dix said enthusiastically. "We have a sculpture very much like it in the large fountain in front of our home. But ours is a Fisch."

"A *Fisch*, really?" Emily replied. "This is a Boxer."

"It looks like a little boy to me," I said.

The two of them stared, Dix frowning at me.

42

Harper laughed. "Boxer is the name of the artist."

"I know. I was making a joke," I said quickly. *Hoo-boy.*

When we arrived back at the house, Gamby was standing at the door.

"Your father's in his office," she told Harper and Emily. "He would like to see you and your guests."

Quinn had told me a few things about Emily's father, Kim Bellaire. Kim Bellaire's mother was Korean, his father a wealthy American. He had met Quinn's dad at Maplecrest, then both went on to Harvard. Kim Bellaire used to play soccer and could still kill you at squash. As for the chain of stores he owned, Kim-Bell's Discount Department Stores, I was already familiar with them: My mother loved to shop for their Bell-ringer Specials.

Emily knocked on the door of the room next to the library, then led us in. Mr. Bellaire kept working, as if he didn't hear us moving about and choosing our seats in front of his desk. I felt like a kid who had been called into the principal's office. Emily and Harper looked around the dark-paneled room the same way Dix and I did—the same way schoolkids do, nervous but curious about the place where Number One spends his time.

The printer was printing. The fax machine was receiving a fax. There was a row of antique clocks on a shelf, each one ticking a different hour.

43

"Eastern, Central, Mountain, and Western time," Dix said proudly, as if he had passed the first question on our exam.

Emily nodded. "London, Seoul, Taiwan," she added.

"Hey, Harper," I said, unable to hide my amazement, "isn't that the Bell-ringer Special bell?" I had seen it for years in ads spread out on our kitchen table, but I'd never known there was an actual bell. It stood about two feet high and appeared to be engraved silver. "Look, it really does have dollar signs in place of G clefs, and musical notes with ribbons tied to them."

Dix smirked.

Okay, it wasn't a Boxer or a Fisch, but it was cool to see—like seeing a place for real after years of looking at it on a postcard.

"Is it solid silver?" I asked.

"Tin," said Harper.

Dix grinned at me. "I guess you've never seen Kim-Bell's jewelry. Not exactly sterling."

As it happened, I had given several pairs of Kim-Bell's earrings to a girl I had dated the summer before.

"I wouldn't exchange that bell for one twice its size and made of gold."

Mr. Bellaire had spoken. We all turned back to him. He had Harper's dark eyes and hair, but was no teddy bear.

"That bell has brought me too much good luck," he added. "I designed it myself, Quinn."

44

"It's great." I resisted glancing sideways at Dix. Looked like I had won myself some brownie points without even trying.

"I'm delighted to have you here as Emily's guest," Mr. Bellaire said, rising to shake my hand.

"Dad, this is Dixon Tully," Harper introduced his friend.

"Ah, yes. I know of Senator Tully."

"Governor, sir," Dix corrected him, smiling politely.

"Governor?"

"Oh," Dix said, as if he suddenly understood. "You were referring to my father, who is the senator. My grandfather was governor."

That Dix was smooth.

"Quite a family," Mr. Bellaire replied, then turned to me. "You don't look as much like your father as you once did."

"That's what people say."

"How's pre-engineering?" he asked.

"Excuse me?"

"Didn't your father tell me you planned to study engineering and physics in college?"

I had tutored Quinn through every low-level math and science course he had taken in the last three years. Was it Quinn or his father who had made up this whopper?

"Yes, I'd like to, if I can keep my grades up," I said.

"How did you do this semester?" Mr. Bellaire asked quickly.

"Fine."

"What were your grades?"

"In the nineties."

"Ninety what?"

Harper shifted uncomfortably in his chair.

"Three ninety-eights, a ninety-nine, ninety-seven, and one hundred."

"You'll keep them up," Mr. Bellaire said confidently. "And what do you all have planned for today?" he asked Emily.

"Maybe riding," she said. "Would you like to come, Dad?"

He didn't answer her. "Are you as good a horseman as your father, Quinn?"

I had been on a trail ride twice, if you counted the mule train with my Cub Scout troop and the pony ring at Little Spurs Ranch. Fortunately, I knew that Quinn wasn't keen on horses.

"I prefer to go by car."

Mr. Bellaire laughed. "That makes two of us."

Then he asked me about my parents. I was prepared for most of the questions, and when I got stumped I was helped out by Dix, whose father was, of course, remarkably similar to Mr. Eaton and Mr. Bellaire, except that he knew the president of the United States. Then a phone call came in and we were dismissed.

"Well, scored a few points," Harper said to me as we returned to the hall.

"Scoring brownie points is one thing," Emily observed. "Lying is another."

46

I turned around quickly.

Her eyes were vivid green stars. "We both know you've won a box of show ribbons," she challenged me.

Apparently Quinn had told Emily and me two different stories about his experience with horses. I wasn't just playing Quinn, I was playing Quinn *in his imagination*. I didn't even know when I was "lying."

"And as for your grades . . . ," Emily went on.

I knew that no matter what Quinn had said in his letters, she'd realize he wasn't a genius—how he said it would tip her off.

"The truth catches up with you," Dix told me.

That was great coming from the King of Fudge. The attitudes in this house were getting to me.

"I earned those grades!" I told her angrily. "Not only that, I've bought Kim-Bell's jewelry," I said to Dix, "when there was a Bell-ringer Special. Any of you got a problem with that?"

Emily flushed. Dix shrugged.

I took a deep breath. I had to shut up. If I wasn't careful, I'd blow it.

"Should I let Tony know when we'll be at the stables?" Harper asked. He didn't seem to like conflict.

Emily turned to Dix. "Do you know how to ride?"

"Well," he replied sarcastically, "I've only won two or three blue ribbons."

We agreed to meet in a half hour, which didn't

give me nearly enough time to get a hold of my pal Quinn and ask him how to get on a horse.

As soon as the horse saw me, he knew he had a sucker for a rider. I glanced up at the saddle. No horn! This was East Coast riding, where if you wanted to hold on to your life, you had better grab a fistful of the horse's mane.

"Is this one going to be all right for you?" Tony asked.

"Sure," I said.

He watched me get on. Emily was several stalls down, whispering to her horse. Dix was off with Harper, trotting around a ring. Trotting—that's one gait faster than I had ever gone.

"You know," Tony said, his big chapped hands stroking my horse's face, "I think I have a better mount for you. Pesto has been kind of grouchy today. Off you go."

Fine with me. I didn't want a grouchy horse. I slid down the side of him.

"Is something wrong?" Emily asked as she led her horse down the aisle. She was wearing skintight riding pants, soft black leather boots, and a thick sweater. Her dark hair was tucked up under a helmet.

"Well!" she said suddenly, her eyes traveling down my blue jeans to my boots. Carville, who had lent me shoes my size, didn't have a pair of boots he wanted me scuffing up. My own boots, which were what I was wearing now, had been through an awful lot of desert, but I loved them. They were decorated snakeskin with pointed toes and heels. "Hello there, cowboy," Emily said.

Tony grinned. "I was just saying I thought the Big B would be a better mount for him."

Emily glanced from Tony to me. "Right," she said. "I'll help you tack her up."

A few minutes later I was up on the Big B, who was shorter and fatter than Pesto. My legs had to stretch more to grip her flanks but, on the positive side, I was closer to the ground.

Tony grabbed hold of my foot, yanking on my heel as the Big B started wandering off. "Heels down," he said. "Heels down. That way, if she stops, so will you."

The Big B followed Emily's horse, whose name was Sofie, on the path down to the ring. I studied Emily's position and mimicked it, sitting tall, feeling taller in the helmet the Bellaires had lent me. *This is pretty easy after all,* I thought. Then the Big B stopped. Just stopped and looked around. At the trees, the squirrels, the little fluff of snow on the grass.

Emily turned around. "Kick her."

I did.

"Harder. Shorten your reins."

I kicked harder. I shortened my reins. The Big B glanced over her shoulder at me as if to say, *You've got to be kidding.*

Then Emily clucked to her and the horse moved on.

49

Okay, now I was in control—kick, shorten reins, and cluck. I could get her started, but how did I stop her? I had thought you were supposed to shorten the reins for that too.

But maybe stopping wasn't going to be a problem. We were at the gate to the ring, which had been swung open by Emily. A nice straw wreath with bright red ribbons hung on the gate. The Big B admired it. The Big B was thinking lunch.

"Pull her head," Emily said as the horse munched away. "Don't let her get away with that."

I yanked. You've heard of headstrong?

"Harder!"

I used all my strength. Her head came around. So did the wreath. For a moment she was wearing it.

Emily collapsed with laughter on her horse's neck.

Dix and Harper rode over to us.

"If you don't like the decorations," Harper said, "just say something, and we'll have them removed."

The Big B pawed the wreath and pulled up a big mouthful of straw.

"Nice boots, cowboy," Dix remarked.

"I like 'em," I replied.

Emily licked her lips, holding back a smile. She looked like the girl who slid down bannisters. "Give us a minute to warm up," she said to the guys. "Come on, heartbreaker."

"Sure thing, Miss Emmy Lou."

She shot me a look over her shoulder.

This time the Big B obediently followed Sofie into the ring.

"How long has it been since you've been on a horse?" she asked.

All of my life, not counting the pony ride at Little Spurs, I thought. "Long," I said.

"We'll trot a bit. You remember posting?" she added. "Up, down, up, down."

I had no idea what she was talking about.

Her horse suddenly broke into a trot. Mine followed. After flopping up and down several times, and hearing the laughter from the entrance gate, I learned posting real quick. Fortunately, my legs were muscular from hockey and other sports; what I lacked in skill, I could make up for somewhat with strength.

"Good," Emily called back to me. "Better," she said.

We circled a couple of times, then joined Harper and Dix.

"How many blue ribbons did you say you won?" Dix asked.

"None."

"Oh." He shrugged. "I must have heard wrong."

"I was just joking about the boxful," Emily interjected, covering for me.

But everyone knew she was covering for me. I felt patronized.

"Em, why don't we take the trail Butter likes?" Harper said.

51

Emily nodded.

"Butter?" I asked. They had put me on a horse named Butter?

"Butterfly," Harper replied. Emily glanced sideways at me. I now knew I was on the old fat horse they gave to children. And we were taking the easy trail.

Harper led, followed by Dix, followed by Butterfly (she was the one doing the driving). Emily insisted on going last—I guess to make sure that I didn't end up somewhere other than the rest of them.

We walked for a while along a wintry wooded path. The only sound was the light stirring of papery leaves and the quiet *thump thump* of horse hooves.

"I like this," I said.

"Do you," Emily replied softly.

We circled around two ponds. The large one had a four-foot waterfall that cascaded into the smaller. Both of them gleamed silver with thickening ice.

"I like this a lot." I glanced back and saw her smiling at me.

"Ready to trot?" Harper called back.

"We're ready," said Emily.

Old Butterfly pricked up her ears as the others moved ahead, then followed suit, lifting her legs, lifting me up out of the saddle. I tingled with cold-air energy.

"Let's canter," Dix called out after about twenty-five yards.

"Not yet," said Emily.

"Why?" I asked, ready to try anything.

She laughed. "Because I said so."

After a few minutes we slowed down to a walk. "Remember, when you canter, you sit deep in the saddle," Emily said to me. "You push down with the horse—you rock. It's almost like a waltz, three beats long."

"Right," I said.

"Are you paying Emily for lessons?" Dix called back to me.

"Depends on how much she charges," I replied.

I was listening to Emily, but I was watching Dix ahead of me, trying to imitate him. He looked great on a horse. Wearing high, polished boots and the same tight riding pants as Emily, he sat tall in the saddle and seemed to control his horse with the slightest pull of his little finger. Harper, on the other hand, though he knew a lot more about riding than I did, looked as if he'd been plopped on. He rode like a sock doll.

We followed a path that was separated from a field by a thin screen of trees. I could feel the rising wind.

"Want to cross over?" Harper asked.

"There's a low stone wall on the other side of the hill," Emily reminded him. They both looked at me.

"How low is low?" Dix asked.

"About a foot, foot and a half," Harper said.

"Can't the Big B step over it?" Dix suggested.

"Yeah, sure," Harper replied. "Just make sure you slow down before you get there, Quinn."

Emily shook her head at him.

"If he's got her down to a walk," her brother argued.

She gave him a look—I think it was one she had learned from her mother.

"It's not a big deal," I said.

"Just make sure you're walking by the time you reach the birches," Harper warned.

"Before then," Emily said quickly.

"Otherwise, hang on tight," Harper advised. "Let's go."

Dix took off first, kicking his horse, whooping. Harper raced after him. They galloped side by side across the field and up a hill.

"Don't be an idiot, Quinn," Emily said, which annoyed me. She eased her horse from a walk to a trot, and I followed. "Lengthen your reins, we'll canter."

It *was* like rocking. Every couple of rocks I got out of sync with the horse, but I finally settled in— rocking, rocking, racing up the hill with the wind in my face, Emily now beside me. It was like a movie, a story taking place a hundred years back, Emily and I riding across the cliffs.

Cresting the hill, I saw the guys far below us, making the low jump.

"Don't be an idiot," Emily called a second time.

My ego was getting a beating.

Emily moved ahead. When she was well out of

54

earshot, I leaned over Butterfly's neck. "Don't be an idiot," I mimicked.

The Big B snorted.

"Exactly," I said. "Let's show 'em."

The birches went by in a blur.

"Slow down!" Emily shouted.

"Pull hard! Hard!" Harper's and Dix's voices rang out.

But I loved the speed, and I knew that Butterfly wanted to make the jump as badly as I did.

"We're gonna do it, girl," I whispered.

Screech!

Well, not *screech*—that's what tires do when a car is suddenly braked—but the effect was pretty much the same. Butterfly stopped. I didn't. For a moment I was airborne, the clouds and field spinning around me. Then everything went black.

Five

I MUST HAVE been out for only a second. I blinked up at a blue and white sky, then heard feet running in my direction. The wind had been knocked out of me, so I lay still, trying to get back my breath and shake off the dizziness.

A beautiful face leaned over me—the face of an angel wearing a helmet.

"Go ahead, Emily," I began. "Say it. You told me not to be—"

"Are you hurt?" she interrupted. "How do you feel?"

"How do I look? Is everything still attached?"

She smiled a nervous smile and touched my hand lightly. "Next time you go over a wall, try it on a horse."

"Good idea." I lifted my head.

"Should he move?" Harper asked quickly. He and Dix were standing behind Emily. "On TV they

56

don't move the victim, you know, in case he's got a broken back—or neck, whatever. If the victim moves the wrong way, *snap*—that's it, paralyzed from the waist down, or even—"

"Jeez, Harper," Dix said, "nothing like scaring him."

"Can you feel your toes?" Harper asked. "Wiggle them, Quinn."

"In these boots? Not a chance." I wriggled my shoulders and lifted my head again. "Nothing's broken, I'm sure. I just had the wind knocked out of me."

Emily slipped her arm very gently under mine. "Take it slowly," she said. Dix helped me up from the other side.

"Thanks, I'm fine," I told them, and walked around, shaking off the pain.

From ten feet away, Butterfly watched me. I climbed over the stone wall and petted her on the neck, then rubbed her soft nose. "My mistake, girl."

"That's a new one," Emily remarked, "a guy admitting to a girl that he's wrong."

I climbed back on the Big B, figuring my tumble was like a car accident—the sooner you got back into the driver's seat, the better.

I told them we should keep going, but the other three said they were cold and wanted to return. I'm not sure they trusted me to stay in the saddle. Dix and Harper rode ahead and picked up speed as they put distance between us. Emily insisted that Butterfly and Sofie walk. Neither of us spoke on the slow trip back. My pride was more bruised than any other part of me, and, as gentle as Emily had been with me, I was a little afraid of what she'd say now that the crisis was over. How long would I be able to get away with my stupid charade, I wondered, before somebody guessed—or I killed myself?

When we arrived back at the stable, Tony and a boy who looked about twelve were cooling down the other two horses.

Tony glanced at my snowy, mud-splattered clothes. Of course, he had already been told the story. By this time, probably everyone in the house would know about my trip over the wall.

"Didn't keep my heels down," I said.

He grinned. "Heard she gave you quite a ride. The Big B hasn't gone that fast for years. Maybe it was that wreath she ate—you know, the one that used to hang on the gate, Mrs. Bellaire's own special creation?"

"That wreath was—?"

"Nah." He laughed and winked at Emily.

Butterfly nosed me softly. I looked into her huge eyes and scratched her behind her ears.

"Why, I think our girl has a soft spot in her heart for you," Tony said. "What do you think, Emily?"

Emily turned away quickly and began to work on Sofie.

"You think our girl has a liking for this one?" he persisted.

"She's just silly enough to," Emily said.

*   *   *

Harper had gotten Mrs. Bellaire's permission for me to use her hot tub and whirlpool, but I retreated to the guest quarters for a long soak. I needed time out from being Quinn.

At noontime, Lonnie brought lunch to my room. "Where don't you hurt?" she asked when I answered her knock. "Shall I come in and set this up?"

"I feel fine," I said, taking the tray from her. "But thanks for bringing it."

"Em and I will be busy wrapping packages this afternoon," she told me. "Do you want a little advice? Don't recover too soon. Harper is dragging Dixon off for his usual last-minute effort to find presents. I've done the shopping other years with Harper, and if I were you, I'd avoid that scene."

I laughed. "I like Harper."

I saw the flicker of light in her eyes. "Do you?"

"He's a good guy. I mean, he's got a good heart. I think he cares about people."

She kept her eyes on my face, as if she was waiting to hear more.

"He's a little clumsy," I added, "but sometimes, when things matter a lot to you, you try too hard and it makes you clumsy."

Her face softened into a smile. "Yeah . . . well, thanks," she said, backing away quickly from the door.

"Thanks for what?" I replied. "You were the one who brought lunch." But I guessed what she meant.

★　　　★　　　★

I spent the afternoon reading my horror paperback. As was the Christmas Eve custom at Deer Hill, there was no official dinner. Fancy sandwiches, a chafing dish of hot soup, and salads were laid out on the dining room table. Both employees and household members were supposed to eat whenever they got the chance. Gamby, Pansy, and I arrived at the same time.

The dog gave me her usual friendly greeting, a couple of vicious growls.

"Oh, hush," Gamby scolded her.

Pansy skulked over to the other side of the room, away from Gamby, but not so far from me. She growled again.

"Dog," Gamby said, rubbing her forehead, which had glitter on it, "get back where you belong. Else I got some ribbon here and we'll make another decoration for the gate."

Pansy whimpered, then trotted through the door that led back to the breakfast room and kitchen.

"She understands English," I said.

"She understands *me*," said Gamby, crunching crackers into sawdust and dropping them into her soup. "Were you told that Mrs. Bellaire wants you all in the hall, looking as holy as possible, not a moment after seven? There's a service tonight in town."

"Yes, ma'am, I know."

That's all we said to each other, except when I offered to take her dirty dishes out to the kitchen with mine.

60

Her eyes narrowed for a long moment. "All right. Don't drop 'em."

"Else I'll be the new decoration for the gate?" I asked.

She grunted. Or maybe that was Gamby's laugh.

At ten of seven that evening I emerged from my room dressed in Quinn's dark suit, a hand-sewn shirt with real cuff links, and a silk tie. If only my mother could have seen me. Over my arm I carried Quinn's cashmere coat.

Dix came out of his room carrying an identical coat, but flung it over his shoulder, holding it by one finger. Oh, we were two classy guys, all right.

"How are you feeling?" he asked.

"Fine. Great."

"I packed some sports cream, the unscented kind," he offered, "in case you're sore. Listen, Quinn, I'm sorry for acting like a jerk."

"When?" I asked, wondering which part of his behavior *he* considered jerky.

"Naturally, I had to take you on," he continued, not answering my question.

We walked down the steps together.

"Take me on? Why?"

"Let me give you some advice," he said, skipping that question too. "Everybody exaggerates some when they talk about themselves. I do all the time."

"No kidding," I said.

"But if you're going to blow something up big,"

he continued, "make sure it's the kind of thing no one will ever catch you on."

It was sound advice for someone in my position, and for a moment I thought he had seen through me. We were walking through the gallery now. I imagined the people in the paintings whispering to one another that I was a fraud.

"Otherwise," Dix went on wisely, "say something halfway between blown up and the truth. If you don't, you set yourself up as a target. How could I have resisted taking shots at you?"

"You couldn't," I agreed.

"Exactly. Well, as they say in election year, may the best man win."

"Win what?"

"Emily," he said.

"But I'm not in the running."

"You're not?" He pulled me back as I was about to enter the drawing room. "Why not? Harper told me you've been writing letters to each other for three years."

"Boring letters," I told him, despite what Emily had said about them. "Nothing more than writing exercises." That was how Quinn thought of them.

"Then why are you here?"

"My parents are in Europe. I needed someplace to stay and I guess the Bellaires thought it was a good idea for Emily and me to meet again."

Dix sat down on a bench, his back to a portrait. A woman in an old-fashioned low-cut dress, sitting primly and holding a small prayer book in her hands, looked over his shoulder. "Just between you and me," he said, "is there something wrong with Emily?"

I shrugged. "She's not easy to figure out. She can go hot and cold on you. But of course she's beautiful and funny and smart. She's . . . well, just not my type."

"But that takes all the fun out of it," Dix complained. "Maybe you'll get more interested in her the more you're around her."

I hope not, I thought. As it was, I was continually reminding myself that I was Jeff Danzig, and therefore not *her* type. The trouble was, to play out the game, I also kept telling myself I was Quinn Eaton. And "Quinn" wanted his chance with her.

"Do you know what I think?" Dix said, studying me. "You really are interested. All you want is to be alone with her. You're just not admitting it."

"Well, I can't tell you what to think," I replied.

He grinned and jumped to his feet. He looked much happier now that he'd convinced himself he still had some competition.

When we entered the drawing room Harper was already there, wearing a dark pinstripe suit, looking much older—even handsome. Only the red and green sugar-cookie crumbs on his lapels identified him as Harper. I signaled to him with my hand. Harper looked puzzled for a moment, then brushed himself off. He, Dix, and I went into the hall.

The Christmas tree was in the center of the marble hall, a mountain of starry lights, rising branch above glittering branch, higher than the second-floor balcony.

"A twenty-four-footer," Harper said.

I turned to him. Lonnie had just come through the dining room door, and his eyes had suddenly shifted to her.

"What kind is it?" Dix asked.

"Velvet," Harper replied.

Lonnie looked incredibly sophisticated in a black velvet dress, her chestnut-colored hair piled up on her head and high heels making her several inches taller.

"I believe the tree is a spruce," I told Dix.

"Nice shoes," Harper said stiffly.

Lonnie glanced down at them. "Thanks."

"And dress," I added. "You look great."

Harper immediately turned away from her and started talking to Dix about their afternoon at the mall and last-minute bargains. Lonnie turned just as quickly to the tree and began straightening and re-arranging ornaments. But I caught them stealing glances at each other. Maybe I could help get them together, I thought. I was feeling rather smug for having figured out their hidden feelings, when I suddenly looked up.

Emily was coming down the steps. She stopped and looked down at me, or Dix—I'm not sure—and for a moment things spun and I thought I was flat on my back in the field again. She also wore a velvet dress. It was the same brilliant green as her eyes, and one side of her heavy black hair was pulled back with a sparkly comb. Something glittered around her throat. I kept looking at her long neck.

"Tell me you're not interested," Dix whispered to me.

"What I said was I'm not in the running," I hissed back.

Emily came toward us.

"Is Mum down yet?" she asked. "Have you been waiting for me?"

"I have," Dix said, smiling at her with the slightest tilt of his head.

I'd seen Quinn do that.

Emily laughed and glanced sideways at me. Like Lonnie, I decided to rearrange the ornaments on the tree.

"How are you feeling, Quinn?" Emily asked.

"Fine. Great. Thanks." I kept my eyes on the tree.

"What are you all doing to the decorations?" Emily inquired.

I glanced at Lonnie for the answer. I was switching balls for no reason except that I couldn't stand watching Dix flirt with Emily.

"Uh, some of these need to hang a little more freely," Lonnie said.

"And you don't want the same colors to hang next to each other," I added with a stroke of inspiration.

"But isn't that what you've got?" Emily pointed to the two red balls I had just placed side by side.

"Oh." I switched them again. There were so many balls crammed on the tree that no matter where I put them, there were still two of the same color adjacent to each other. I gave up. Where was Mrs. Bellaire and her stuffy conversations when you needed her?

"Look at that ornament," Dix said. "Is it a family joke?"

"Which one?" Harper asked.

Dix pointed to an angel that had chewed-up pencil legs, a round body—I think it was a painted piece of a toilet paper roll—sagging wings that were crusty with glitter, and a fuzz of black wool hair.

Lonnie lifted the angel down. "There really isn't enough room on the tree for this."

"That's mine!" Harper protested.

"Harp, look at it," Lonnie replied reasonably. "It's ready for the trash."

"But it's always looked this way," Harper argued, taking it out of her hands.

Emily laughed softly. "See, there's mine," she said, pointing higher on the tree. "Lonnie made us those when we were little."

Harper rehung his angel. Lonnie watched, then lowered her soft gray eyes.

"Harper, please keep your hands off the tree," said Mrs. Bellaire, coming down the step. "Some of those ornaments are worth quite a bit of money." She paused for a moment, taking us in. "My, don't you all look smashing," she said. She slipped into a full-length mink that Mr. Dove had brought in for her.

"You look smashing too, Mum," Emily said. "And Mrs. Dove. Is that new?"

Mrs. Dove was following Emily's mother down the steps, wearing a plaid wool coat with a huge corsage pinned to it.

"A Christmas gift," she said proudly. "Robert picked it out."

"Your father won't be coming with us," Mrs. Bellaire told Emily and Harper. "Last-minute details on a business deal. You understand."

"We understand," Emily repeated. I caught the sharp edge in her voice.

"The car is ready," Mr. Dove told us, and we all filed out after Mrs. Bellaire.

Later that night, when I was lying in bed and most of the big house was dark, I thought about the tone of Emily's voice, how it could suddenly get sharp—and unhappy. During the car ride to church, the cool mask had slipped over her face again, hiding whatever she was feeling. It surprised me how much I wanted to know what she was feeling, and to know whether I was part of the world she thought about.

Throughout the service she looked like the prim and perfect daughter of Mr. and Mrs. Bellaire. Dix, sitting next to Emily, had continually glanced around the church, commenting to her on the architecture and the people. Finally Mrs. Bellaire had given him a sideways look, and he became devout. Lonnie, sheltered between Emily and Mrs. Dove, had prayed her heart out. Harper had spent the time looking down at his clasped hands.

I turned over in bed, pushing off the quilt, and stared out the window at the piece of moon sliding down a starlit sky.

Harper and Lonnie, Dix and Emily, and my-self—I sure hoped somebody got what they wanted for Christmas.

Six

I N THE DREAM I was nine years old again. It was the first Christmas after my father had left us, and I had made a dozen little decorations out of wood pieces for my mother, hoping that, wrapped separately, they would somehow make up for the fact that he wasn't there. I arranged them carefully beneath a two-foot plastic tree with blinking lights. My mother was baking cookies. She had opened all the windows of the little apartment, for Christmas was sunny and hot in Phoenix that year. She smiled at me, but her eyes were red from crying. The kitchen timer went off and she walked away quickly. It kept buzzing—it was my morning alarm.

I reached over to flick the tiny switch on the clock. Sitting up, I looked around the room of pale silk stripes. Frost etched the long sets of window-panes. Outside the morning was gray, but small white lights jeweled the bushes in the courtyard below. The window candles in the main house had been lit, pane after pane shining with a soft glow. The homes Emily and I came from couldn't have been more different.

At nine-thirty I met the others in the dining room for Christmas breakfast. Mr. Bellaire joined us, wearing his reading glasses, a pen clipped onto his red sweater. Emily gave both her parents a shy kiss. Her father patted her hand lightly. Harper shifted uncomfortably from foot to foot.

"Harper," his mother said quietly.

He gave her a quick kiss on the cheek.

"Merry Christmas," Dix said, shaking the Bellaires' hands, and mine too. We took our seats at the table.

Mr. Dove began to serve us crepes. You know, those pancakes that are thin as paper and wrapped around fruit and stuff.

"So, Quinn," Mr. Bellaire said, "I was hoping we'd hear from your parents."

I gulped my orange juice. That's all I'd need, for the Eatons to phone Deer Hill. My voice was several tones deeper than Quinn's.

"I called them early this morning," I replied. "They send their good wishes to everyone." It was what Quinn had instructed me to say. In England, it would already be Christmas afternoon. I hoped Quinn had remembered to phone them before they phoned me.

"We were delighted to hear from your parents,

Dixon," Mrs. Bellaire said. "Weren't we, Kim?"

Mr. Bellaire grunted.

"We look forward to meeting them this afternoon," Mrs Bellaire went on. "Your sister as well."

Mr. Bellaire looked at his wife over his glasses but said nothing.

"How fortunate that they are passing through on the way to your ski house," she added.

Mr. Bellaire stabbed his strawberry crepe.

Mrs. Bellaire continued. "Your mother said that with election year coming up for your father, he very much needs a break."

"Not to mention financial contributions," said Mr. Bellaire.

Emily's mother ignored the comment. "It must be very exciting to campaign, Dixon. Do you help out?"

"Oh, yes. I enjoy working with the aides and getting out to meet all the voters," he said, putting down his fork, leaning forward. "But more important, I am proud of my father. I believe in my father."

I glanced sideways at Mr. Bellaire.

His eyes rose from the mangled crepe to meet mine. "And you, Quinn? Do you also believe in your father?" He had a way of pinning you to the chair with his eyes, making it hard to lie.

My father would be spending Christmas Day with his tribe of children and probably several of their mothers, merrily handing out paper plates with turkey and dressing, and napkins that said

71

Happy Halloween because they were cheaper than the Christmas pack.

"In some ways more than others," I replied.

Mr. Bellaire laughed and nodded. Without meaning to, I kept scoring points with him.

But I couldn't tell if anyone was scoring with Emily. She wore that cool and polite expression I was becoming so familiar with. It was tempting to make faces at her from across the table.

After breakfast we went to the drawing room to open gifts. Quinn's silver-and-gold packages had been added to the pile. You could tell which gifts were from the Bellaires—the wrapping paper was color-coordinated with the room furnishings. There was another pile, wrapped in heavy white paper and real velvet ribbon—Dix's, I figured.

I began to get really nervous as Emily worked her way through her mound. She kept bypassing the gifts I had brought. I knew that Quinn had gotten her a black-and-white silk scarf and something called a Coach bag, which he had described as "a cross between a gym bag and a purse, and ridiculously expensive." They weren't my gifts, and she wasn't my girlfriend, I reminded myself, but I wanted her to like them.

She opened them last. "My," she said, "how useful."

I nodded. Having been furious with Quinn for apparently leading her on with romantic letters, I was now furious with him for buying such unromantic gifts.

72

Dix, who had brought gifts for everyone in the family, including Pansy, had given Emily a gold chain. She put it on now, then turned to him.

"How does it look?" she asked.

"*You* look beautiful."

She smiled at him.

I saw Harper taking mental notes. But I knew that he was even more hopeless than I was. We could memorize all the good lines we wanted, but actually saying them to a girl was something else.

I continued to unwrap the haul of gifts I'd be bringing back for Quinn, sweaters and cuff links and an all-leather sports bag like the kind the guys at school carried. The phone rang, and I stopped ripping paper.

"Are you expecting a call?" Harper asked.

"No," I said quickly.

Someone must have picked it up in another room. I waited for Mr. Dove to come in and announce that the Eatons were on the phone. He didn't.

Get a grip, I told myself. More than a hundred people had been invited for open house at Deer Hill that afternoon. A few phone calls for directions and last-minute excuses were bound to come in.

"Did you get something for Lonnie?" I asked Harper.

"Yeah. It's pretty cool," he whispered, as if she were in the room.

"Well, what is it?"

"A toolbox."

"A *toolbox?*" Like I said before—he was even more hopeless than I was.

"An emergency kit for her car," he explained. "She drives an old Toyota back and forth to college. It's got everything she'd need if she breaks down somewhere."

How useful. Poor Lonnie.

"Now everyone must put away his or her own gifts," Mrs. Bellaire said, her voice rising over ours and the rattling sound of Pansy burrowing through the wrapping paper. The dog had greeted me with an unconvincing snarl. Maybe we had a truce for Christmas.

"The staff is much too busy today to tend to such things," Mrs. Bellaire went on. "And please be ready in your best by one o'clock."

I had just gathered up Quinn's loot when Lonnie entered the room. She was dressed in a black uniform with a starched white apron.

Harper smiled at her. "Are you helping out today?" he asked.

"At the beginning of the party, until some part-timers arrive," she replied, but she kept her eyes on me. "You have a telephone call. It's your friend Jeff."

"Huh?"

"Your roommate from school."

"Oh. Jeff."

"Maybe you'd like to take it in the library," she suggested, and led the way.

When we got to the room, she pulled a piece of

paper from her pocket and said softly, "Your parents called."

"My parents? When?" I asked, panicky.

"While you were opening gifts. I told them you weren't available at the moment."

Close one!

Then I looked at Lonnie curiously. She knew the Eatons were calling from Europe—it seemed odd that she wouldn't have fetched me immediately.

"They said they had to switch hotels. Here's the phone number where they can be reached."

"Thanks, Lonnie."

She nodded and left, closing the door behind her.

I picked up the phone. "Hello?"

"It's me," Quinn said. "Listen, we've got a problem. I can't get through to my parents."

I gave him the information Lonnie had given me.

He sounded relieved. "I'll try them now. I hope they're there, I hate missing time on the ski slope. See you—"

"Wait!" I said. "I've got a question."

"Can you make it quick?"

"Yeah. It's about Emily. She runs hot and cold, but when we're alone . . . what I want to know is, did you ever say anything real romantic to her?"

"I guess it depends on what you call real romantic."

I groaned.

"I mean I may have practiced a few lines," he said.

"Nice of you to remember now."

"You're a true friend, Jeff," he said. "I promise, when we get back to school, I'll set you up with a terrific girl. I've already got someone in mind for you."

"Can't wait," I replied unenthusiastically.

The library door opened.

"Oh, hey, here comes Emily now," I said. "It's my friend Jeff," I told her.

"Hi, Jeff," she called out.

"She sounds normal," Quinn said quietly into the phone.

"Jeff says hi."

"Too bad about the way she looks," Quinn went on.

"Jeff says he really, really wishes he could stop by to see you," I told her.

"I'd like to see him too," Emily replied, and sat down on the leather couch, pulling up her long legs.

"Too bad she's so unfriendly," Quinn remarked.

She was wearing the same outfit she'd had on at breakfast, those stretchy pants girls like—they clung to every curve—and a very loose, open-necked sweater.

"Her parents should never have sent her to that strict convent school," Quinn continued.

But something looked different now: The sweater was off one shoulder.

"Yeah," I agreed. "If only they realized the effect it's had."

"Well, hang in there, buddy," Quinn said. "I promise I'll pay you back."

"Merry Christmas to you too," I said, hanging up.

"Your best friend?" Emily asked me.

"No. My roommate at school."

"Oh. That's right. I think you mentioned him in a letter," she said. "The megabrain. The guy who studies all the time and never has a date."

I have dates! I almost shouted back.

She patted the seat next to her. "Do you have somewhere else to go, Quinn?"

"I guess not." I sat down next to her. "Jeff—my roommate—he dates," I told her, "but there's no one around that he's interested in during the school year. He likes the girls at home."

"What I want to know is who you like," she said.

I avoided her eyes and ended up staring at her bare shoulder. I had an overwhelming desire to kiss it.

"Oh," I said, "I'm an easygoing guy. I pretty much like everybody."

She shifted her position and looked at me, her head tilted. "When am I getting the Christmas gift you promised?" she asked.

"When would you like it?" I asked back, hoping for some clue about what had been promised.

She laughed. "Right away! Though waiting for it is nice too."

"Is it?"

"I've waited a long time for you to kiss me."

Not on her shoulder, I told myself firmly. I leaned forward and kissed her lightly on the forehead.

She looked up at me, her eyes shining, then shut them, her dark lashes sweeping down. I didn't shut mine—I was memorizing each of her features.

Then I kissed her, very, very gently on her cheek, almost touching her mouth.

"That's it?" she asked after a moment. "That's what I've been waiting for?"

"Uh . . ."

Go for it, whispered a little voice inside me. *Don't be an idiot. She's gorgeous. She's waiting.*

"That's my Christmas kiss?" she exclaimed with disbelief.

But she was waiting for *Quinn,* and when I left Deer Hill, the real Quinn would never show up. She'd be left with a broken heart.

"Are you afraid of me?" she asked.

"Afraid? Of course not."

"When you touched me, I thought you were trembling."

"I wasn't," I insisted.

We stared at each other for a long moment. My heart was banging like a sledgehammer. I wondered that she couldn't hear it.

"Okay," she said, standing up. "My mistake. Merry Christmas." She was mad. "May all your secret dreams come true."

Seven

JUST BEFORE ONE O'CLOCK I called my mother out in Seattle. The phone rang and rang before it was picked up.

"Is Kate there?" I asked.

The person at the other end let the receiver drop. A moment later my mother came on.

"Who was that?"

"Aunt Bet's night nurse. The day nurse hasn't shown up yet," Mom explained. "It's so good to hear your voice, Jeff." Her own voice quivered for a second. "Are you having a good time?"

"I guess. Yeah. It's interesting. But I miss you," I told her.

"I miss you big time, honey!"

"Did you open your present?" I asked, then turned my head away from the phone. I thought I heard someone outside my bedroom door.

"I adore it! Adore it!" my mother replied. "But Jeff, it's too expensive—"

"Just keep adoring it," I said. "It'll look great on you."

I had gotten her a huge turquoise pin. Quinn thought it was tacky, but I knew it would be perfect for Mom's rodeo queen outfit.

"It does look great. I'm wearing it now, I love it so. It's hard— Well, you know how clingy mothers can get. This is the first Christmas you haven't been home."

"You're not clingy. It is hard."

"Are you sure you want your gift sent to school?"

"Positive."

"I wish you were here," Mom said, "but I'm glad you're there, if you know what I mean. Love you."

"I love you too," I told her, then held the phone away from my ear. I was sure I heard something brush against the wall outside my room.

"Uh-oh," my mother said. "The other nurse has arrived. I've got to go play referee. See you when I see you, honey."

"Bye."

As soon as I hung up, I went to the door and yanked it open. No one was there.

The only thing that the Bellaires' party was missing that afternoon was a narrator, some guy with a British accent to explain what was about to

80

occur in the upcoming episode; I mean, the event looked just like something I'd seen on PBS. A trio played string instruments in the center hall. The large hearths in the drawing room, dining room, and library crackled with fires. Candles flickered inside tall glass globes, and silver trays gleamed in the hands of people who were dressed in crisp black and white and moved quietly among the guests. Even the Bellaires' friends laughed and talked as if they all had watched a lot of *Masterpiece Theatre*.

On the outside, I looked as if I belonged. On the inside, I felt like a guy who had wandered in accidentally from a network sitcom.

"Mingle," Emily told us. "Mum said we have to mingle and be gracious—you know, chat people up."

"Delighted!" said Dix. He started off, then glanced over his shoulder at me. "Come along, Quinn, let's show them what absolute charmers we are."

For the next hour I let him do the talking while I nodded and sneaked peeks at Emily from across the room. She was wearing a short red silk dress that got a few inches shorter whenever she moved. She was mingling at the moment with five guys ranging from our age to the midtwenties—guys who owned the duds they were wearing, guys who probably drove little sports cars, guys who had more money than I could earn in a hundred summers at Burger King. I watched them out of the corner of my eye, waiting for the wall of dark jackets to part and my chance to see that short red hem go up and down.

Harper, meanwhile, was eating cake with an elderly lady who kept tapping him on the arm as she talked, causing his fork to wave dangerously.

Eventually I got a break. A little kid struggling with a piece of pie launched it across the hall's smooth marble floor. I wiped up the mess before any of the waiters could get to it and used the dirty napkins as an excuse to retreat to the kitchen.

Gamby, the afternoon's field general, took the sticky linen from me.

"Any need for a dustpan or soap?" she asked.

"No, ma'am. Floor's clean."

Mrs. Dove looked up from the double stove and smiled at me.

"Merry Christmas, Mrs. Dove," I said.

"Stand clear," Gamby barked, which made me jump directly into the path of a waiter. We did a little dance around each other, but he managed to keep his tray upright.

"I guess I should go back to the party," I said apologetically.

"All I said was stand clear," Gamby grunted.

Mrs. Dove winked, then nodded in the direction of the table against the wall. Maybe Harper also came out here for breaks, I thought. I went over and sat down. A large box lay open on the table: a Garber Tool Kit, Lonnie's gift from Harper. Figuring Lonnie wouldn't mind, I started looking through it. "Wow," I said quietly. "Wow!"

I knew what I wanted for next Christmas.

"I'll swap it for that soft blue sweater you got."

I looked up at Lonnie and grinned. "This really is good stuff," I told her. "Top quality. It's a Garber Kit."

"Yeah, can't wait to use it," she said.

"You can only get these at Garber stores or through their mail order," I explained to her.

"Really?" She whistled with mock appreciation.

"Do you know the stores in the nearby mall?" I asked. "Do they have a Garber's there?"

She shook her head. "I know Greenside from end to end, all three levels. I've never seen it."

"There you go," I said triumphantly.

Lonnie looked at me, puzzled.

"Harper might have done all his other shopping at the last minute, but he bought this gift earlier. He had to plan this one. Don't you get it? He thought about what he was giving you."

Her gray eyes lightened a little, then she looked down. "I see. He thought that, like the other guys he knows, I'd really love this. He'd give it to his best friend, so he gave it to me. Well, that's nice," she said. "I mean it. Really." Her smile was un-convincing.

Poor Lonnie. Harper would have done better by filling a box with Bell-ringer Specials instead of these expensive tools.

"Actually, Lonnie, guys don't buy tools for other guys," I told her. "Tools are very personal things."

"Personal?" She picked up a wrench. "Think I could hang it on a chain?"

I grinned at her.

"And what's this thingamajig?" She opened up a battery cleaner. "Oh, a mascara brush."

I laughed.

"How about this?"

"WD-40. It's a lubricant," I told her.

"For my elbows and heels, I guess. Oh, *yes!*" Lonnie pulled out a pair of protective goggles and put them on. She looked like a bug.

"Smashing!" I said, and this time she grinned with me. We searched the box for other usable tools, our heads close together, laughing. When we looked up, Emily was watching us from across the kitchen. She didn't crack a smile.

"Em!" Lonnie called. "Come here. See what Harper gave me. A real treasure chest!"

Emily came over, looked down at the tool kit, then sighed. "I knew I should have dropped some hints. I meant to write to him from school—"

"Don't worry about it," Lonnie said, taking a screwdriver and poking it through her hair, which she had twisted up on the back of her head. "It wouldn't have made a difference. Harper doesn't pick up on hints."

"I've been trying to convince Lonnie that your brother put a lot of thought into his gift," I said to Emily.

She glanced up at me, then smiled at Lonnie. "*Les goggles sont très chic.*"

The three of us started laughing.

Emily sat down.

"A mascara brush," Lonnie said, showing her. "A pendant."

"Nice," Emily replied. "Oh, look at these." She held up two valves. "You'll have to get your nose pierced, Lon."

"Pierced? Nah, why not just use—"

"Rubber cement!" they shouted together, and laughed as if it was hilarious.

I didn't get it.

"It's an old joke," Lonnie told me. "You see, when we were little girls and liked to play with hair—"

"And jewelry, and makeup," Emily said. She paused. "Actually, it started with two old Barbies and some scissors and glue."

"But it was much more fun working on each other," Lonnie continued. "We discovered that paste was okay, but rubber cement worked better."

They dissolved into laughter.

"Mum was not pleased," choked Emily. "I guess you had to be there."

They laughed even harder.

"Lonnie." It was Mr. Dove calling her. "We really do need your help now."

"Oops," she said quietly. "Coming!"

The three of us got up reluctantly. Lonnie started off, but Emily caught her arm. "You want to save this for a fancier occasion," she said, removing the screwdriver from Lonnie's hair. Lonnie was still giggling as she ran off to assist her father.

I turned to Emily. "Have you two always been friends?"

Emily nodded and smiled. "We grew up together. Lon is two years older than I, so there was never a time for me when she wasn't around. She knows more about me than anyone."

"And you know more about her—I guess it works both ways."

"It used to," Emily replied. I heard the wistfulness in her voice. She slipped the screwdriver into the box and picked up another tool, but she wasn't really looking at it. "I guess both Harper and I got used to Lonnie always being here for us. I know, I know—talk about selfish!

"Lonnie's very smart," she continued. "It's good that she's away now. It's just that it's not as comfortable as it used to be. There's a kind of distance between us now."

"It didn't seem like that a few minutes ago," I observed.

Emily smiled again. "There are still times when it feels like it used to—now and then." She glanced at me and her smile turned sly. "Like when we talk about you."

"Oh."

Her eyes were twinkling. "Why are you so shy when we're face-to-face, and so, well, anything but that in your letters?"

I glanced around the kitchen uncomfortably. What kind of "anything but" had Quinn written to her?

She took my hand and pulled me toward a closet, opening the door.

"I'm claustrophobic," I protested, looking over my shoulder to see if anyone had noticed.

"It's a stairway, stupid." The narrow back stairs ran up to the second floor. "Close the door behind you," she said.

I did, then followed her.

We emerged in the upstairs hall between the music room and the master suite. Emily started down the hall in the direction of her and Harper's bedrooms.

I took a quick detour into the music room. No one else was there, but it had been decorated and there was a tray of cookies laid out on the piano. I hoped someone would show up soon.

Emily glanced back at me. "See what I mean?" she said.

"See what you mean about what?"

She laughed. "Okay, you stay there. I want to get something."

I shifted from foot to foot. I didn't know why I was so afraid to be alone with her. Maybe because it would be too easy to convince myself that Emily would rather have a holiday romance with "Quinn" and never see him again than none at all.

Emily returned carrying a box decorated with butterflies. She opened it and pulled out papers that looked like correspondence.

"Would you please sit down?" she said. "You're making me nervous."

I sat down stiffly on the piano bench. "You get a lot of letters," I remarked.

"You write a lot of them," she replied.

"I wrote all those?"

She cocked her head at me.

"Uh, it's just that it doesn't seem like it," I said. "I guess because writing to you comes so naturally, I hardly realize I'm doing it. Could I see them?"

"Why?"

"I'd like to remember what I said."

She frowned. "If what you said was important to you, you'd remember."

But I'm playing Quinn, I felt like arguing, *and nothing is truly important to Quinn.*

"Okay," I said. "Read me your favorite." *Give me a clue,* I thought, *some hint of what is supposed to be between us.*

"'October twenty-first. Dear Emily—It's midterm week, so I have been up long hours—'"

Well, that was true, though Quinn hadn't been up studying.

"'—and not one hour has passed without me thinking of you.'"

Hoo-boy.

"'I long to hold you in my arms and never let you go. I want to shower you with tender kisses. I want to taste your sweet lips and feel your hands caressing me.'"

"Cripe!" I said. "That *is* romantic."

"Why are you surprised?" she asked sharply.

"Surprised?" My voice cracked a little. "I guess

it's just that it sounds really romantic when *you* read it, you know, when you read it out loud."

"You didn't write this, did you?" she said accusingly.

I blinked. Now what? Should I confess quickly, beg for mercy, treat it like a joke—though it wasn't a joke to me—or make one last effort to convince her?

"What makes you say that?" I asked, trying to sound indignant. "Of course I wrote them."

"You didn't," she insisted.

I was about to give in.

"You got someone else to write them for you," she said.

"What—What do you mean?" I sputtered, trying to catch up with her thinking. Was that all she suspected? "I wrote every word myself."

Whatever those words were. I wanted to kill Quinn.

She pulled out another letter.

"'December sixth. Dear Emily—It seems as if I have waited forever to pull you close to me, to wrap my trembling arms around you. I have waited forever to encircle your tiny waist in my shaking hands, to feel your smooth back—waited forever to feel your throbbing heart pressed against mine, beating wildly.'"

I found myself taking long, slow breaths, inhaling, exhaling, the way I do before a big hockey game.

She put down the letters and sat down next to

me on the piano bench. It was just big enough for the two of us. "So how come you keep waiting?" she asked.

"Well," I said. "Well—" I leaned back and accidentally banged my elbows down on the piano keys.

Emily jumped at the sound, then laughed and put her arms around me.

"I don't really know," I said, which was true. She made me all mixed up—one minute she was hot, the next minute cold. I couldn't figure her out. And I couldn't help wondering what it would be like to kiss her. There wasn't a guy in this world who wouldn't want to know—why not go for it?

She reached up and turned my head toward her, drawing my face down close to hers. I stared at her lips, the soft little pucker at the top. My hand went up to touch her head. I had one finger twined in her beautiful hair. We moved closer, closer.

"Miss Emily."

Mr. Dove again. We both drew back.

"Miss Emily," he said, his voice clearly carrying down the hall, "are you up here?"

Emily moved quickly over to the other chair and started gathering up her letters. "Yes, Robert."

He stood in the doorway. "The Tullys are arriving. Your mother wishes you to be present. You as well, sir," he said to me.

He saw her stuffing the letters in the box and

came in to take it from her. "Shall I put this in your room, miss?" he asked, neatly closing the lid.

"Yes, thanks. Thanks for your trouble in fetching me."

"Not at all, miss." He nodded formally. "Emmy," he said, his voice suddenly soft. He touched the tip of his ear, then flicked his eyes toward me on the piano bench. Her sparkling earring lay in my lap, caught in a fold of my jacket.

I quickly handed it to her.

Only Mr. Dove left the room without blushing.

Eight

EMILY AND I arrived at the foot of the large curved stair a moment after the Tullys came into the entrance hall. Mrs. Bellaire glanced sideways at the two of us but said nothing. Dix greeted his family. Harper stood behind him, holding on to Pansy, who was struggling in his arms.

"Hello, you sweet thing," cooed a pretty girl with short, spiky blond hair and a bushy fur coat.

Harper looked at the girl, a funny smile on his face.

"Is she friendly?" the girl asked.

"Oh—you mean Pansy? Usually, but I'd better hold on to her," he replied.

"Okay." The girl smiled up at him with large mascara-darkened eyes, then moved very close to pet the dog. "I'm Tracy, Dixon's sister."

Harper looked over her head at Emily and me,

his own eyes round with wonder. Emily started to giggle.

Meanwhile Dixon was introducing his parents to Mr. and Mrs. Bellaire. It looked as if the Tullys had photocopied themselves to make their kids: Mrs. Tully was petite and blond and wrapped up in a huge coat like Tracy, and Dix had inherited from his father the tall, dark-haired good looks that I was pretty sure girls and women went crazy over.

"And this is Emily," Dix said to his parents.

Mrs. Tully extended her hand, then gave her a little kiss on the cheek. "Emily, we meet you at last," she said, as if they had heard about her for years.

The senator shook Emily's hand, smiling widely, then winked at Dix. Emily had won his seal of approval.

"And this is, uh . . ." Dix gestured to me. He couldn't remember my name. For a moment, with "Jeff" on the tip of my tongue, I couldn't remember either.

"Quinn," said Mr. Bellaire, who was standing in back of our group with his hands jammed in his pockets, as if he were trying to keep his money from leaping into the senator's campaign fund.

"I think—I think Pansy likes your coat," Harper said to Tracy. The dog was licking it.

"It's a fake, Pansy," Tracy said. Her accent was much more southern than Dix's; either she added to the drawl for effect, or Dix had worked hard to eliminate his. "It's just plain fake," she continued.

93

"So is Mother's. We're for the environment. We'd never wear *real* animals."

Mr. Dove stepped forward then, and the Tullys' fake animals were carried off to coat hangers.

"It was lovely of you all to invite us," Mrs. Tully said. "Tracy was feeling lonely without Dix around to tease her."

"You mean to *torment* me," Tracy corrected her mother. "Don't let it go to your head, Dixie," she said to her brother as she continued to pet the dog.

Harper didn't seem to know where to look, especially since Tracy had shed her furry bear look to reveal a tight-fitting sweater dress. Her gold chain and heart-shaped locket rode up and down, up and down—well supported, if you know what I mean. She leaned toward the dog and Harper backed up against the wall.

"Oh!" everyone said at the same time as the big chandelier and wall sconces blinked off.

Emily and I reached behind Harper's back at the same time to turn the lights back on. Our hands touched and she smiled a little.

"Thank you," Mrs. Bellaire said, with the tired sigh that touched her voice whenever Harper was around, then she led the senator and his wife off for a tour and introductions. Mr. Bellaire made some excuse about tending to other guests. Harper clung to Pansy, as if the dog were the magic charm that drew Tracy to him.

"I believe I need to comb my hair and put on a

touch of lipstick," Tracy said, glancing from Harper to Emily.

"No, you don't," Harper said enthusiastically. "You look great."

Tracy laughed.

"You can use my room," Emily told her, taking her arm. "Come on, I'll show you the way."

As soon as they disappeared, Dix turned to Harper. "Well?"

Harper stared down at Pansy, scratching her ears.

"You like her," Dix said.

"She's kind of cute," Harper replied, then glanced up at me. "Don't you think?"

"Sure, if you like cold, wet noses," I said. "Oh—you mean Tracy."

Dix glared at me.

"She is cute," I said. "Sort of like a cheerleader."

Dix's eyes narrowed. "She's not a cheerleader. She's president of her class and plays varsity sports. She started her school's volunteer tutoring program and works in the community recycling center. She was this year's chairperson of the junior prom. Do you want to know more?"

I shook my head. "No, thanks. You've said enough to tell me she's out of my league."

It's not that I disliked Tracy; I just didn't want to see her cheerleader looks distracting Harper and breaking Lonnie's heart on Christmas. Having been distracted by a few cheerleaders in my own life, I knew how easy it was.

"I've got to get rid of this dog," Harper said. "I think I'll lock her up at the Doves'. Where's Lonnie?"

"I'll find her," Dix said quickly, taking the dog from Harper. "You wait here for my sister."

I watched him work his way through the crowd, trying to carry Pansy without getting hair or drool on his jacket.

"Petits fours, gentlemen?" a server asked Harper and me.

I lifted a little cake from the silver tray. Harper picked up two napkins, lined his pocket, deposited in it several icing-covered cakes, and took one more to eat right then. The server moved on as if he had seen nothing unusual.

"Quinn, what kind of guy do you think Tracy likes?"

"I don't know. I think she might like you," I replied honestly, reluctantly. "Of course, I could be reading her wrong. I don't know her any more than you do."

"Yeah, but you're experienced," Harper said. "You're successful with girls."

"Not really," I told him, weary of the charade I had to play.

"You know," Harper went on, "I still have friends at Maplecrest. When I heard you were coming, I asked them about you. I mean, I'm Em's brother, I've got to watch out for her," he added defensively.

"Of course you do," I replied, wondering what

96

exactly Harper had been told about Quinn. "But you also know the rumors about my blue-ribbon achievements with horses."

He laughed a round, deep laugh. "Yeah, that's true. Still, I've seen you with my own eyes—I've seen the way Emily looks at you."

"How does she look?" I asked quickly.

Not that it matters, I reminded myself; *she's looking at "Quinn." She's flirting with the rich guy who wants to shower her with tender kisses and taste her sweet lips and feel her hands caressing him, the guy who has been waiting forever to feel her throbbing heart pressed against his, beating wildly. I couldn't have written or whispered that to her in a million years. Still . . .*

"How does she look?" I asked again.

"Oh, you know, you've seen it before," Harper replied. "What kind of guy do you think Lonnie likes?"

"Tell me, tell me first, Harp, how—"

"I'm being dense, I know," he continued, pulling a cake out of his pocket. Little dark threads were stuck to the icing. "I mean, the answer's obvious. Lonnie would never like the kind of guy Tracy likes. And anyway, I think it's Pansy that Tracy really likes. She would never be interested in someone like me. Would she?" he asked, clearly hoping against hope.

I sighed. "You're consulting the wrong person. I honestly don't understand girls. There's just one thing I know from experience, Harper: Never say never."

"What do you mean?"

"Girls specialize in confusion. When you've finally got one figured out and know exactly what to do next, she'll turn everything around on you. Nothing is ever the way you thought it was."

"Why?" he asked. "That doesn't make sense to me."

"If it did, you'd be a girl."

That night I felt as though I were sleepwalking the last ten feet to my bedroom. The big house was silent, but I could still hear people's chatter ringing in my ears and smell the darkened fireplaces and burnt candles.

"If I'm not up, bang on my door," Dix said as he stumbled past me in the hall.

I set two alarms so I'd wake up in time to get ready for our trip to New York City the next day. Across the courtyard, the windows in the Doves' wing were dark. Lights were going out one by one in the main house, where Tracy and her parents were staying. They would be leaving for Vermont early the next morning. I crawled into bed, snapped off the light, and closed my eyes.

It was like walking into a movie theater. As soon as the darkness enclosed me pictures leaped up in front of my eyes, larger than life. I drifted in and out of a troubled sleep. Scenes and conversations from the day replayed themselves. My eyes opened. I was wide awake and full of questions.

How did Emily look at me? How would she

look at me if she discovered that her rich, romantic guy was an imposter who had never uttered a mushy word in his life and would have to scrape to buy her a Bell-ringer Special? How did *I* look at *her?* Could she read in me the feelings I didn't want anyone to know?

I tossed and turned for an hour, then decided to find the cupboard in Mrs. Dove's kitchen that had all the good stuff to eat. Tying Quinn's robe around me, I tiptoed along the hall, then felt my way down the steps.

The stone house was cold. The moonlight in the portrait gallery paled the painted faces, making them watchful ghosts. The drawing room seemed even larger in the dark, its corners receding into blackness. Here and there, objects glinted—the teapot, an andiron, a doorknob. From the center hall came a warm glow. I walked silently to the doorway.

The tree was on, a shimmering tower of green and red and gold. Sitting on the floor, leaning back against the staircase and wrapped in a large quilt, was Emily. She cradled Pansy in her arms and stared at the tree, unaware that I was watching her. Her face was shiny, reflecting the tree's light. She had been crying.

I wanted to ask her if she was okay. But with all the guests and workers coming in and out, and being stuck with me for most of the holiday, I thought maybe she needed this time by herself. I was about to retreat when Pansy growled softly.

Emily turned around quickly, then held the dog up to her face, wiping away the tears. For a moment neither of us said anything.

"I—uh—couldn't sleep and was on my way to raid Mrs. Dove's cupboard," I told her.

She smiled a little. "Dovey would be pleased if you did."

"I guess you couldn't sleep either," I said tentatively.

The dog growled.

"Oh, hush, Pan." She put her hand over its little muzzle. Pansy shifted into whines of disapproval.

"I didn't mean to disturb you," I added, and started to turn back.

"Aren't you getting something to eat?" Emily asked.

"Uh, that's okay. I'm not really hungry now."

"Saw me and lost your appetite," she remarked.

"What?"

She pulled herself up taller. "If I promise to protect you from my vicious dog," she said, "would you like to sit and look at the tree?"

"Uh . . . sure."

"You sound so enthusiastic," she commented.

"Well, I just thought you might need some time to yourself."

She spread half the quilt on the floor next to her, as a place for me to sit, and set Pansy down on the other side.

We sat arm to arm and gazed up at the tree in a long, uncomfortable silence.

"Did you want to pick up where we left off this afternoon?" she asked. "I mean, up in the music room?" Her voice was neither inviting nor dissuading.

"No."

"Well, you sure know how to keep a girl from getting a big head!" she exclaimed.

I swung around to face her. What did she expect me to say? She had been crying a few minutes before. "Do *you* want to make out?" I asked her.

"Right now? No. But you know guys, they always—"

"Uh-huh," I cut her off.

"I guess I just wanted you . . . to want to," she said quietly.

"So you could say no!" I felt totally frustrated.

She shook her head. "I just wanted you to—to *want* to," she repeated, then sank down in her blankets, like a little kid sinking down behind her school desk after giving an embarrassing answer.

I rubbed my head, half angry, half feeling bad for having jumped at her.

"It's an awesome tree," I said, gazing up at it.

"Yes."

Another long silence. She had her side of the quilt pulled up around her, as if for protection.

"Do you sit here often?" I couldn't think of anything else to say.

"All the time when I was little," she said. "I used to lie under the branches and look up. I'd imagine it was a whole forest, a mountain of fir trees."

I started to smile.

"I'd dream about exploring it," she said, "following paths through its branches. The lights were stars, and the balls this fantastic kind of fruit. And there's a copper tiger we hang up every year—he was my hunting companion. Well, you know how kids imagine things." She mumbled the last sentence.

I had done the same thing as a kid, even with our two-foot plastic fir. Now I crawled over to the big tree and lay down on my back beneath it, looking up.

"The long silver icicles," I said, "could be little rivers, streams cascading down the mountain."

She didn't say anything.

"I see a candy house. Did you and your tiger sleep there at night?" I asked.

"Once. Only once. We found out it's really the home of a witch."

"How'd you get away?"

"Lonnie-Angel saved me."

I raised my head off the floor to look at her. Her face glowed softly in the dark, reflecting the golden light of the tree.

"Lonnie-Angel, the one with the chewed pencil legs?"

"Yes. Do you like the big tree at Rockefeller Center?" she asked.

I lay back down again. "Never seen it."

"Never? I mean the one next to the ice-skating rink in New York."

"Oh. That one. I've never seen it close up," I fudged.

"I've always wanted to skate beneath it," she said softly.

The marble floor beneath me was freezing. I slid out from under the tree, then sat up next to her. We struggled for a moment with the quilt, me trying to wrap it around her and her trying to pull it around me. "Stop making things difficult," she said.

We wrapped it around the two of us like a giant cocoon. "How come you never did—skate under the tree, I mean?"

"Every year my dad would promise to take me."

"But he was always too busy."

She nodded.

"I guess your parents are busy most of the time."

"All the time. But they give me everything," she added quickly. "Everything. I know I'm stinking rich and lucky."

For a moment that statement stuck in my gut. I wouldn't mind being stinking rich. "Right," I said. "But is there anything you really want that they don't give you?"

"Like what?"

"Like . . . time. Time to take you skating. Time to find out what you're doing, what you're thinking." I shrugged. "That kind of thing."

I saw her swallow hard. "They haven't a clue. They don't care. Not at all."

"I don't believe they don't care—" I began.

"They love a girl who doesn't exist, their own

perfect creation. The worst part is I've played along. Now I'm trapped inside this Emily who's a fake.

"I nod and smile and say little meaningless things," she went on. "I pay ridiculous compliments to ridiculous people, playing nice-nice to snotty ladies and their daughters. Half the time today, what I really wanted to do was throw a pie in their faces."

I laughed. But then I saw there were tears in her eyes.

"I'm a fake. As fake as the Tullys' coats." Her voice dropped to a whisper. "But I'm afraid to be anything else."

"Why?"

"If I say what I'm really thinking and do what I really want to do . . . " She bit her lip.

"They won't love you?" I guessed.

She pressed her lips together tightly. "I keep trying to get it right, to deserve what I've been given, but the more I do, the less I feel like Emily."

"But what about Lonnie and Harper? They know you, the real you, don't they? And they still care."

She looked at me, a flicker of light in her eyes.

"Trust them. I think you have to trust yourself and your own sense of who you are, but if you're feeling kind of unsure right now, trust the way *they* love you."

Her green eyes were wide and thoughtful.

"I'm glad you came," she said at last, then snuggled close to me. "You must miss— You must miss your family. No matter what, everyone does. But I'm glad you came."

104

I put my arm around her, holding her next to me beneath the quilt. A few minutes later, her body got heavy against mine and I knew she was asleep. Pansy settled down and made little snoring sounds. For a long time I held Emily and gazed up at the glittering tree. I didn't want to awaken her from such a peaceful sleep, but I could feel myself getting drowsy.

"Em," I said quietly. "Emmy." I shook her gently and her eyes opened. "You need to go to bed. Come on. I'll help you up."

"The tree," she said sleepily.

"I'll turn it off," I told her, "after we get you up the steps."

I rolled up the quilt so she wouldn't trip on it and put it under one arm, her under the other. We took it one step at a time, Pansy following us, her tags jingling. At the top of the stairs I wrapped the quilt around Emily like a stole. "Can you make it the rest of the way okay?"

She nodded silently.

"G'night."

I turned to go down the steps, but she stopped me. She caught my hand in both of hers, hesitated, then lifted it and very lightly, very shyly, barely touching my fingers, kissed them. She let go quickly and disappeared down the dark hall, the little dog trailing behind.

When I glanced down at the tree, the starry lights blurred for a second, my eyes unexpectedly wet.

Nine

NONE OF US made it down to breakfast in time, so Mrs. Dove packed up fruit and bagels to be eaten during our trip into the city. Since no one else was around, Dovey let me cut the pats of butter and fold the napkins. While we worked, she told me Emily had invited Lonnie along.

"Which was kind—Emily is always kind," Mrs. Dove said. I could see that something was worrying her.

Mr. Dove had brought around the limo, but the others were still getting ready. I went to the library, the only room in the main house with truly comfortable chairs. Two cookies from the day before had been left on a table. I was munching on one when Tracy came in.

"Good morning," she said cheerfully.

"G'morning."

She sat down in a chair that was positioned at a close right angle to mine. "I'm Tracy."

I nodded. "Quinn. We met when you first arrived."

With her spikes of blond hair, short green skirt, and tights, she looked kind of like Peter Pan. Peter Pan with curves, that is.

"Oh, yes! But you know," she said, touching me lightly on the wrist, "I met so many people yesterday, I can't keep everyone straight. Where is it you said you came from?"

"Maplecrest Academy."

She laughed. "No, silly," she said, "I meant where is your primary home?"

"Rhode Island," I answered for Quinn.

"I *knew* you were a northerner. You have houses in other places, of course. . . ."

"Of course," I lied.

"And what is it that your daddy does?"

"He's a businessman."

"I can't quite remember what it is he owns," she prompted sweetly.

"Mink ranches."

She blinked. "Pardon me?"

"You know, places where they raise minks and sew them into coats."

"Oh."

Actually, Quinn's father owned ships.

"Well, New York City is wonderful this time of year," she said, changing the subject.

I nodded. "I'm sorry you can't go with us. What

107

time are you and your parents leaving for the ski house?"

"They've left."

"Without you?"

"I'm staying *here*," she said, touching me on the knee.

"Really? Terrific," I replied. *Poor Lonnie,* I thought. "For how long?"

She shrugged. "I'm going to see how it goes. Mother and Daddy are entertaining some VIPs— political folks—and I'm just so glad to be away for a bit. Mother gets kinds of pushy when the pressure's on."

"I see." I picked up the other leftover cookie.

"Oh, you don't want that," she said, catching my hand. "Breakfast is already packed for us."

I smiled at her. "I've got room for breakfast."

"But that's not good for you."

"It's Christmas," I said. "You're not supposed to eat what's good for you."

"It's stale," she said, catching my hand a second time.

"I like them stale."

She cocked her head and studied me.

"Why don't we go see if the others are ready?" I asked.

As soon as we stood up, I popped the cookie in my mouth.

Emily and Lonnie were standing in the hall, admiring the new clothes each was wearing—their Christmas gifts. Emily had on jeans and a short leather jacket, creamy beige, so soft it looked like velvet. Her hair was in one of those long plaits—I think it's called a French braid. Lonnie's hair was tied back in a big bow.

"You forgot your screwdriver," I said, and she laughed.

Emily acted the way she always did when we were with a group of people. But this morning, the polite distance she kept seemed to me more like shyness than coolness.

Harper and Dix showed up and we all piled into the limo. I sat on one side of Harper. Tracy wedged herself in on the other side. "It's just a teeny bit tight," she said.

Harper, proving that he, even more than I, belonged in dating school for the pathetic, tried to give her more room. Quinn would have lifted his arm, draped it over the seat, then let it slip down to her shoulders.

"I'll go up front," Lonnie volunteered.

"Don't bother, I will," I told her.

"I said that I will," she insisted.

"I'm on my way," I said, bumping my head against the ceiling.

"I often ride up front," Lonnie told me in a low, firm voice.

"So ride in the back for a change."

Emily's head went back and forth, as if she was following a tennis match.

"Live dangerously," I went on, "ride next to Harper."

109

I pulled Lonnie into my seat.

"I took a shower this morning," Harper assured us.

"And we're all glad for it," said Dix.

I closed the back door. When I climbed in next to Mr. Dove, who was pretending he didn't hear any of this, I saw that Harper had thoughtfully made room for Lonnie, so there was a large gap between his shoulder and hers, none at all between him and Tracy. Getting the right people together was hard work.

Mr. Dove dropped us off at a fancy hotel called the Plaza and agreed to pick us up there at five-thirty that evening. Emily had a phone in her purse to call him if we wanted him earlier.

"What should we do first?" Tracy asked. "Stores, a ride in the park, the Angel Tree at the Met?"

"Stores," Dix said.

"F.A.O. Schwarz," Harper suggested.

"I just love that place!" Tracy exclaimed.

Emily remained quiet. I wondered if we were anywhere near her tree at Rockefeller Center.

We shopped in stores where a suitcase cost enough to pay several months' rent on our Phoenix home, then moved on to designer clothes, where labels were everything. Emily purchased a soft gray sweater. Tracy kept pulling Harper over to look at this and that, telling him what she just loved. I guess she didn't know that Harper was slow to take hints, and if she didn't watch it, she might end up with a tool chest.

I was glad to get to F.A.O. Schwarz. The price tags were just as unbelievable there, but they sold toys, and toys had labels that I was familiar with, like Mattel and Disney. The store was packed, and we moved along the aisles like people at a museum exhibit. At the stuffed animal department I watched Emily cuddle a floppy-eared dog. Dix was watching her too, probably thinking the same thing as me—that a dog's life could be pretty good.

Lonnie sorted through the toys, looking for a turtle. "That's what our team is called at Maryland," she said. "The Terrapins."

"Here's one," said Emily.

Lonnie held it up and laughed at its smiling turtle face. "It's great," she said, flicking the price tag over. "I like its fat little feet," she added, then put the expensive toy down.

Tracy was pressing a stuffed pony to her—well, to her cheerleader curves. "I had one just like this when I was a little girl," she said.

And Harper bought it. I mean he *bought* it— not just the line, the pony.

"It's your Christmas present," he said gallantly. "After all, I didn't give you one. Do you really like it, Tracy?"

"I love it to death," she said, squeezing it tightly against her.

Lonnie glanced away.

It took us an hour to get through the store,

so the brisk air felt good when we emerged.

"Let's do the park," Dix said. "I'll treat you to a carriage ride," he told Emily as we crossed the street.

The old-fashioned carriages were lined up at one end of Central Park, their hoods decorated with holiday garland and brass lanterns tied with red bows. Bells jingled on the horses' leather. The horses did not look as cheerful, however. They hung their heads, blowing clouds of steam through their nostrils and stamping their feet on the hard surface of the road.

"Does this bother you?" I asked Tracy.

She looked at me blankly.

"The horses," I prompted. "Does it bother you as an animal rights person?"

"But this is what horses are for," she said, "pulling us around."

"They're certainly well cared for," Dix remarked, petting the nose of one.

They didn't look that way to me.

"I need to walk," Lonnie said. "What if I meet you all back here?"

"Do you mind if I walk with you?" I asked.

"What?"

"I don't want to go in one of these," I told her.

"Well, then you shouldn't," Emily interjected. She sounded a little miffed.

"Would you take this for me, please?" Tracy asked Lonnie, handing her the F.A.O. Schwarz bag with the stuffed pony. "I'd die if I lost it."

"Sure."

"Is there a reason why *you* can't carry it?" I asked Tracy.

Lonnie quickly shook her head at me.

"You can put it on the floor of the carriage," I continued, pulling the package out of Lonnie's hand, giving it to Harper. "See you in a half hour. Come on, Lon."

I pushed her by the elbow and we headed into Central Park without looking back. For the first few minutes neither of us spoke, which was just as well. I was getting really annoyed with some of the attitudes I'd been seeing, but as Quinn, I had to keep my cool. It turned out that Lonnie was pretty aggravated too. With me.

"What gives you the right to mess with my life?" she said angrily. "What gives you the right to play matchmaker?"

"What?"

"I know what you're doing, and I'm telling you to stop it." She hurried down the park path with long, determined strides.

"Lonnie?"

"Just keep your nose out of my business! You don't understand how it is."

"I understand how you feel about Harper," I replied. "And I know I don't enjoy seeing you treated like a personal servant."

She swung around. "There are things you know nothing about! Things you're acting stupid about!"

I circled around a guy trying to sing carols to

113

the beat of a percussion synthesizer and caught up with her.

"Things like what?" I said. "If you're going to yell at me, I'd appreciate it if you'd be specific."

"Like Harper and me." She was crying now. "Like employers and the children of employees. Like lines between social classes that can't be crossed."

I grimaced. I should have known—I had heard it before at school.

"And how to drink tea without getting the cup stuck on your finger." She started laughing through her tears. "And how to get on a horse. I wish you could have seen Tony's imitation of you."

"Sorry I missed it."

"And, if you must bring along your holey shorts and T-shirt, how to make sure the servants don't discover them."

"What are you saying?" I asked her suspiciously.

"What's your real name?"

I stood still. "My—?"

"I mean the one on your birth certificate," she said.

We faced each other.

"Jeff."

"Jeff." She nodded. "It suits you."

"How long have you known?" I asked her.

"Pretty much from the beginning."

"What?" I exclaimed.

She began to walk, but this time at an easier pace.

114

"I suspected from the time Emily told me about your noble struggle with the teacup. Then my father mentioned how you tried to help him with the luggage. And, well, there were lots of little tips along the way."

"I've been that obvious? Why haven't the Bellaires said something? Emily knows?"

"Oh, don't worry about the Bellaires," she said. "Or the Tullys."

A skater rolled between us, then a bicyclist streaked through.

"It's just as my father has always said," Lonnie went on. "You can't fool the servants."

I must have been keeping them all amused in the kitchen.

"Domestic help are trained to read faces and body language," she continued. "A good domestic fetches what the employer wants before it's even asked for. Even though I'm not technically a servant, I often get treated like one. That way?" She pointed.

We stepped through a broken piece of snow fence and crossed a grassy area.

"People aren't careful about what the servants see, any more than they're careful about what a lamp observes. So we see plenty of slipups."

"Hoo-boy."

"How do you know Quinn?" she asked. "You can't really be roommates."

"We are. I'm at Maplecrest on scholarship. I, uh, guess you're wondering why I'm subbing for him."

115

"He got a better offer," she said matter-of-factly.

"Right. He's skiing at Killington. How'd you figure?"

"I met Quinn three years ago, when Emily was still going through miserable adolescence and I was just emerging from it. He wasn't so hot himself, and he was *very* easy to read."

We reached a thinly wooded area and started clambering over rocks.

"Good thing Emily wasn't trained like you," I remarked.

"Well, I'll tell you," she said as we puffed our way up a huge slab of black rock. At the top we both sat down. I could feel the rock hard and cold through my jeans. For the first time since I had left Maplecrest, I felt as if I was on solid ground. I felt like me.

"Emmy is busy reading other things into your actions. Which means you should stop paying attention to me," Lonnie warned.

"Why? I'm not flirting with you," I said. "Anybody can see that. I'm helping out. You deserve a break."

"That's nice of you. But what Emily sees is you teasing me in the kitchen yesterday, you giving up your seat in the car for me today, you wanting to walk alone with me in the park—get it?"

"But you've fallen for Harper, and she must know that."

"She doesn't. And neither you nor I can tell

116

her. Believe me, the line can't be crossed, Jeff—especially when you live in the same household."

"Says who?"

"It's how it has always been," she insisted.

"But what if Harper has fallen for you?" I reasoned.

She laughed, but there was no happiness in her face. "Be real. Even if Harper was willing to break the rules, I'm not his type. I am not short, blond, and cute."

She put her hands behind her and started sliding down the rock.

"You mean Tracy. That's nothing, Lonnie." I landed on my feet next to her. "She's flattering him left and right—just the way she gazes up at him is adoring and sweet—and in the beginning guys always fall for that. But in the long run they figure things out."

"Harper and I have known each other since my mother was pushing us in a double baby stroller. How much of a long run does he need?"

We walked in silence for a while.

"To be fair," Lonnie said, "I myself didn't realize it at first. I always wanted to be around him, always waited for him to come home from boarding school, but until last year, I thought it was a sister-brother thing." She shook her head. "I don't know how he became something else for me, I never meant him to be. Anyway, bottom line is, it can't be," she concluded.

I wanted to argue with her.

"And I need to get away from Deer Hill," she said, "the sooner the better. We should start back, Jeff. I have no idea where we are."

We tried one path, then backtracked and took another, finally finding ourselves on a main road through the park.

"You know, when you're gone, they'll miss you," I said to her.

"I guess Emily will."

"Emily already does. She told me it's not the same between you."

Lonnie nodded. "I know. It's hard to be close when I'm keeping my biggest secret from her. I wish it weren't that way." Then she smiled a little. "Did you notice what size sweater she bought today?"

"No."

"My size."

"It was a soft gray—just the gray of your eyes," I said.

"I'm going to have to fuss with her when we get home," Lonnie told me. "Em has always bought me things—with her own money, not her parents'. I don't think her parents know. I know they didn't know about the tickets she bought so that Gamby and Tony could fly to Naples to see their family last summer. The airline folder mysteriously appeared one day, and Mrs. Bellaire didn't look too pleased when Gamby thanked her for her generosity and thoughtfulness. I found the receipt when I was cleaning behind Em's bureau. There's a lot you don't know about her."

We stopped for a moment to watch three guys on in-line skates, performing for a small crowd.

"It looks as if Emily's got everything, but she pays a price," Lonnie said. "She's expected to be a perfect reflection of her parents—a mirror that always makes them look good. When she feels like she can't, when she feels down and afraid, she goes to my mom. We're almost sisters from sharing a mom."

I remembered Emily's comment when she saw the photograph of my "teacher": *Her face is nice—she looks like a person you can talk to.*

The guys on skates collected money in a hat and rolled away.

"Ever done that?" Lonnie asked. "Ever skated?"

"I was the best street hockey player in my neighborhood." It felt good to say true things. "I play ice hockey now at Maplecrest. When you can fake around broken concrete as well as players, it's a cinch to do it on a smooth rink. I'm hoping that hockey and grades will help pay for college. I'm on the same side of that line as you."

"Mmm."

"Not that it matters," I added. "If Emily is jealous, it's for the attention of Quinn, not me. Quinn of Eaton's Shipping, Inc."—I grimaced—"and writer of incredibly romantic letters."

"Are you sure? I think there may be hope."

119

"As you told me before, be real."

"What's real for you, Jeff?" she asked. "How do *you* feel?"

I kicked at a stone. "Like the sooner I get away from Deer Hill, the better."

Ten

W E ARRIVED BACK at our starting point just before the carriage did and saw it coming around the curve in the road. The driver in the top hat was pointing out something and the four of them in the back were talking and laughing. Dix had his arm around Emily. Tracy gazed up at Harper. They looked like an ad for the Office of Tourism: *Come to New York. Find out how romantic the holidays can be.*

The driver jumped down from his perch and offered a hand to Dix, who leaped lightly to the ground, then helped out the two girls. Harper's turn was next. He reached the pavement with unexpected grace. It was as if Tracy's attention had given him the confidence he needed.

"So it's all set," said Dix. "I'll call Mother tonight and tell her to expect the five of us. You ski, don't you, Quinn?"

"Yes." I didn't ski anything like the real Quinn did, but I had gone three times to Flagstaff with a friend of my father's.

"And how many blue ribbons did you get for skiing?" Dix goaded me.

"You mean *hats*. Gloves. A dozen of those. The other skiers never saw me coming."

Harper laughed. "Glad to hear it. You're going to make me look good."

Lonnie glanced with surprise at the new Harper, a guy who seemed suddenly at ease with himself.

We crossed over to the circle in front of the Plaza, then headed down Fifth Avenue. Music tinkled from shop fronts, and the pungent smoke of roasting chestnuts hovered at the street corners. The sidewalks were packed with window-shoppers, some of the crowd edging out into the street.

"I'm sure Mother won't mind. It will be for just one night," Tracy said. "Of course, the guest rooms will be occupied, but the five of us can camp out on the living room floor."

"It's s—" *Six*, I was about to say. "Never mind."

"Six. Lonnie's coming, of course," Emily said, but her voice was a little cool. Maybe she did think I had a thing for Lon.

"She skis better than any of us," Harper added enthusiastically. "But I've been out twice already. We'll see this time," he said, grinning at Lonnie.

"I'm sorry, but I can't," Lonnie told them. "I have some things to do before I return to school."

"It's just one day, Lon," Harper argued. "We'll

go up tomorrow evening, ski Sunday, and return Sunday night."

"I'm sorry, but—"

"But you've got other things to do." Harper's voice had an edge. "I guess you want to get back to all your friends at Maryland."

Lonnie nodded and looked away.

"Some of the people in the pictures I saw. I guess you're missing Tom."

Lonnie didn't reply.

"Where did you say we were going?" I asked.

"To my parents' condo in Vermont," Dix replied. "We call it Capitol Haven."

"It's at Killington," Emily told me.

"Killington?"

Lonnie and I exchanged glances.

"It's a huge resort," Lonnie said quickly. I guess she saw the panic in my eyes. "It's actually six mountains that are connected. There are miles and miles of ski trails, and a zillion people."

What were the odds of Emily running into one good-looking skier always on the make, who'd eagerly introduce himself as Quinn Eaton? A zillion to one didn't seem safe enough.

"Everybody is wearing hats and goggles, so everybody looks the same," Lonnie added, trying to be reassuring. "You'll have lots of fun."

"Then everything's settled," Tracy said, taking Harper's hand. "Oh, look." She pointed across the street. "I need to stop there."

I gazed up at a cathedral, but it turned out that

Tracy was pointing to the next building—Saks.

"Looks like we're at Rockefeller Center," Dix said.

The place where Emily's tree was. I glanced around. A long inlet of pavement ran between buildings, its center planted with some twiggy-looking angels. At the end I saw a square of brightly colored flags and another tall building.

"It's down there," Emily said, as if reading my mind.

"I think this is the year," I told her.

Her eyes grew bigger. "You really want to?"

"I need to—" Tracy broke in.

"Then just do it!" Emily told Tracy. "Come on, you." She pulled my hand.

"Where are we going?" Dix asked irritably.

"To Saks," replied Harper.

"To the skating rink," said Lonnie.

Dix followed Lonnie and us.

"Don't get any ideas about me, Emily," Lonnie said on the way. "I want to watch, not skate."

"You're actually skating?" Dix said. "Isn't that kind of a touristy thing?"

When Dix saw the price of renting skates, he called it outright robbery and refused to do it. Maybe he was cheap. Maybe he thought it was good for our "competition" if I had a turn with Emily. Or maybe he couldn't skate and had more sense than I did when I tried to ride Butterfly. He and Lonnie returned to the observation deck.

The rental skates were not only expensive but

lousy, with edges like old scissors. Still, just lacing them up felt good. Skating was something I knew. Skating made me feel like me.

"I'm not good at this," Emily confessed. Her face was luminous as a candle. It seemed to me as if everybody around us should notice, and every guy want to skate with her. "I'll probably fall flat on my behind. I guess I should have told you that before."

"Doesn't matter. I'll keep you upright," I said, "and if I don't, I'll go down with you."

She smiled.

When we emerged into the daylight, I heard Emily draw in her breath. The ice rink lay in a plaza maybe twenty feet below street level. A glass-enclosed restaurant was next to it, its small trees winking with lights. The big tree rose up several stories, glittering, pointing upward like the tall buildings that surrounded the plaza. Above us, spectators in colorful winter jackets lined the railings, looking down into our Christmas garden world. Some kind of waltz was playing—it sounded like a music box.

"Ready?" I asked.

She nodded.

Our first lap was slow and careful. Emily said she wanted to skate by herself, and I gave her the room she asked for. She made two more circles and began moving with more certainty. I skated behind, listening to the music, enjoying the feel of ice beneath my feet.

Then she slowed and held out her hand. It wavered.

"I don't want to trip you," she said shyly as I grasped her hand.

"Just skate. I'll worry about where our feet are."

"You're good at this, aren't you?" she said, glancing up at me. "You do this a lot?"

"Yeah, but holding on to a hockey stick, not a girl."

My feet matched the stroke of hers.

"Which do you prefer?" she asked.

"You're warmer."

It was so easy. It was as if I had skated with her all my life.

Sometimes I could feel her looking up at me, other times I caught her with her head back, looking up at the tree as we glided by. She reminded me of a little kid on a swing, leaning back to look at the sky.

"Whoa!" she said, suddenly straightening up and seeing a kid flying in our direction. I lifted her arm and the boy went scooting underneath. Emily began to lose her balance and I whirled her around. It was like a turn in a dance.

"Nicely done!" I said.

She was laughing and laughing. "I'm just hanging on tight," she said.

Our feet found the rhythm of the music. It felt as if no one were skating but us, as if we were the only ones moving through a still landscape of people. I turned and skated backward, facing her, pulling her with me, unable to take my eyes from hers. Now it seemed as if we were still and the world was rushing by.

I don't know how long we skated like that—two laps, ten laps—before the human cannonball found us again. There was an audible gasp from the crowd above us and the next moment the three of us were flat on the ice.

"You okay?"

"Why don't you guys watch where you're going?" said the little boy.

Emily was laughing, her hands up to her cheeks.

I helped up the kid, then her. Her laughter made her helpless.

"You're like spaghetti," I said, pulling her up.

The hour of skating flew by. By the time we were finished, Harper and Tracy had rejoined Lonnie and Dix, and we ordered a late lunch at the rinkside cafe.

Afterward we went up to the Metropolitan Museum of Art to see the Angel Tree and nativity scene. My moment of magic was over, for Emily now stuck very close to Lonnie. Dix and I walked around with our hands in our pockets, trying to look like two cool guys. Tracy and Harper spent a lot of time in the gift shop.

When Mr. Dove picked us up, Lonnie immediately got in the front seat. I ended up next to Emily in the back. It started to snow as we left the city. The bridge lights were fuzzy blue stars. Emily fell asleep. Whether by plan or by accident, I didn't know, but her head rested against my shoulder. I wanted Mr. Dove to drive on and on.

I couldn't believe that I was falling for Emily. Had fallen, I corrected myself. I'd been hooked from the moment I saw her sliding down the bannister.

Lonnie turned around, saw Emily asleep, and winked at me.

"I've been thinking, Harper," Lonnie said softly. "A day of skiing is too much fun to miss. Can I change my mind and go?"

Come to New York, I thought. *Find out how romantic the holidays can be.*

Eleven

IT SNOWED ALL night and most of the morning. I began to hope we wouldn't make it to Killington. But the Bellaires had their own snowplow, and the main roads were clear enough by five P.M. This time Emily insisted on riding in the front seat.

"She sure is sending a lot of mixed messages," Dix whispered to me. "Do you have any idea which of us is ahead?"

"I told you before, I'm not—"

"Yeah, right," he said. "I noticed that yesterday." He actually looked pleased with me.

The trip was slow because of the weather and we didn't get to the Tullys' condo until nine-thirty. By the time we warmed up dinner and cleared a space for sleeping in the living room, it was time for bed.

"Full day tomorrow. No partying now," Senator Tully said, smiling at us.

Not that there was a chance—Mr. Dove was

129

occupying one of the sofas. We unrolled our sleeping bags within the rectangle formed by two short sofas, one long one, and a raised hearth. Emily and Lonnie lay head to head closest to the fireplace, then came Dix and Tracy, then me and Harper. Mr. Dove, having checked us over like silverware laid out on a table, nodded and turned out the light.

The remains of a fire hissed in the fireplace and disintegrated into gold flakes. Outside, snow slid off the roof. No one spoke. I was soon asleep.

It seemed like one minute later when I opened my eyes and saw pale pink light painting the wall. I lifted my head to look around.

"Morning," Lonnie called softly. She pulled herself up on her elbows.

"Anybody else awake?" I asked, just as quietly.

She shook her head, her chestnut hair catching the early light.

"Lonnie, I've been wondering, how come you changed your mind?" I asked. "How come you came?"

"I don't know." She thought for a moment. "I suppose because you've been there for me the last few days. I figured I'd be here for you. And maybe I hoped a little, after our trip to New York. You never know how things might turn out for you and me. It's crazy, I know," she added quickly.

"It's not crazy," I said.

"We'd better not talk now," she whispered.

I nodded and we both settled down. When I

130

awoke the second time, the room was white with sunlight. Dishes clattered in the kitchen, and bacon and coffee smells drifted in.

At breakfast we looked at a map of the trails. Lonnie had been right. A complex web of colored ribbons covered the terrain. There were double chairlifts, triple chairs, quads, gondolas. I counted six base lodges, with cafeterias, restaurants, lounges, shops, and parking. The chances of meeting up with Quinn had to be small.

Our skis were loaded on the car. I was the only one in our group without a pair, and by the time I had rented some from a lodge shop and was buckling up my boots, we had all grown sweaty inside our thermal clothes. "Ready at last," I said, and rose from a bench.

At the same time, a guy across the room straightened up. We stared at each other for a moment. Then I saw him check out the people I was with, his eyes resting on Harper, who, even in his ski clothes, was recognizable.

"What are *you* doing here?" Quinn mouthed to me.

The others had started toward the lodge door.

I held up a single finger. "One day," I mouthed back, hoping Quinn would realize we were there for the next eight hours and he should lie low for that time.

"Come on," Emily said, turning back to me. "Don't the boots feel right?"

"They're fine." I thumped behind her.

When her back was turned again, I glanced to the right. Quinn was staring at Emily. I knew he had caught only a glimpse of her—he couldn't see her shining hair up under her hat and the long, beautiful neck that was wrapped in a scarf. Still, there was a look of wonder on his face.

We followed the others to a lift line that would take us to the top, where trails spoked off in different directions. The runs ranged from difficult to easy.

"Double black diamonds," Dix said as he and I rode up together. "We have several choices of black diamond trails from this peak. Which do you want to try first?"

According to the map legend, double black diamonds indicated the most difficult trails, those with very steep gradients. Single diamonds were a little less difficult. Blue was moderate. Green was easy.

"You choose for yourself," I said. "I'm doing green."

"You're not," he said in disbelief.

I didn't reply.

"I wonder what trail Emily will take," he mused.

I got his point. My sense of daring wasn't the kind of thing to inspire female adoration. On the other hand, Maplecrest's hockey team had a lot more games to play, and I was working for a college scholarship. I needed both legs.

"Guess you'll have to ask her," I said.

At the top of the mountain the temperature was several degrees lower and the wind blew hard, snatching our breath away. The six of us huddled together.

"Double diamonds!" Harper repeated after Dix. "On the first run? No way."

Harper kept surprising me—showing some courage then, being the first of the group to nix a macho proposal.

"Harper's right," Lonnie said. "We shouldn't start any higher than blue."

Emily and Tracy nodded.

"That okay with you, Quinn?" Harper asked graciously.

"Sure. I'll meet you at the bottom. I'm taking green."

"Gr—" Harper shut his mouth quickly. I guess he remembered what had happened the day I "proved" I could ride. "Okay."

One by one the others started down a blue-marked trail. I trekked over to a route where a lady with a million wrinkles and a hat that looked like an aviator cap was digging in with her poles. She smiled at me. "Cheers," she said, then took off.

I gave her some distance and followed. It was a great trail, with long, easy loops. *Swoop, swoop*—I felt so free, snow rushing under my skis—*swoop*—wind whistling around me—*swoop*—big paint-brush arms of pines coloring the edges. Snow, trees, sky, sky, trees, snow—that's all there was. For a moment the world seemed clear and simple.

Swish!

Suddenly a skier passed so close to me that I felt his windy wake.

"Jerk!" I shouted.

Her wake. She skidded to a hockey stop at the edge of a trail.

I skied over and made a slow stop beside her. "Emily, what are you doing?"

"I wanted to ask you the same question," she said, "though not about skiing."

"How'd you get here?"

"A connecting trail," she explained.

"The others are going to wonder what happened to you."

"Here's what I'm wondering," she said. "Have you fallen for Lonnie?"

I looked at her, amazed. Lonnie's instincts had been right.

"No, of course not."

She didn't look as though she believed me.

"What makes you think that?" I asked.

"Oh, come on," she replied. But it didn't come out sounding nearly as certain and casual as she wanted it to.

"Well?" I prompted.

She looked self-conscious. "The way you—the way you look out for her."

"I can care about someone without falling for her. I can try to help a person without being in love with her."

"True." She wasn't going to argue with me, but I could see she wasn't convinced. "Okay." She glanced over her shoulder, then started off.

"Emily!"

I skied after her. You know what they say about wings of love. She made a nice, easy transverse of the hill, like you're supposed to; I went flying straight down, cutting her off.

"Jerk!" she yelled.

We skied apart, like a zipper opening, then veered together again, ending up tangled in a snow-bank off to the side.

"What are you doing?" she demanded, pulling her skis apart from mine.

"Trying to get you to use your brains," I said.

"You just about knocked them out of me."

Snow covered her hat and scarf. She pulled her goggles off.

"Listen to me, Emily. Lonnie's having a tough time."

"I've known Lonnie a lot longer than you," she said quickly. "I know when she's unhappy."

I waited.

"And you're right, she is," Emily admitted. "But she won't talk to me about it. Lonnie has always told me what's going on. We could tell each other anything. She won't talk now. And the only thing I could think was that she's fallen for you."

"No," I said firmly.

"But she said she started hoping after the trip to New York and—"

"You were awake this morning?"

Emily clapped her mitten over her mouth.

135

I laughed. "You were eavesdropping. Well, Lonnie's hoping, all right," I said. "Hoping for Harper."

"What?" Emily's eyes grew wide.

"Why do you think I was trying to cheer her up about the tool chest he gave her? I knew she had fallen for Harper. Then Tracy came along, flattering him and treating Lonnie like a personal servant. It made me mad. Lonnie's hurting. Her feelings seem obvious to me. I don't know why you can't see it," I added.

"I—I guess I just never expected it. Harper," she said, laughing softly.

I'd never felt so warm sitting in snow.

"You know," she went on, "I once thought Harper had a bit of a thing for Lonnie, but that was last year, maybe two years ago, and he never did anything about it."

"Could he have?" I asked. "Lonnie's convinced that Harper can't cross the line between him and her. Like it's not proper or something."

"It's not," she said.

"You don't really believe that."

"I do."

"That's stupid. That's prejudice!"

"It's the way it is, though," Emily replied calmly.

"Only if people agree to it," I said hotly. "Only if they let it be that way."

She just looked at me.

"I think Lonnie's too good for Harper," I remarked. I wasn't sure whose battle I was fighting,

Lonnie's or mine. After all, we were both on the wrong side of the money line.

"Maybe so. It probably happens a lot that way," Emily said.

Well, now I knew where she'd stand if I told her the truth about me. Too bad, not fair, but that's the way it was. I could barely contain my anger. But I was Quinn, and Quinn couldn't have cared less about this kind of thing.

I pulled myself up and offered her a hand. Not that I wanted to—I felt like skiing off and leaving her in a pile of snow.

"Don't be angry," she said as we checked our skis. "Please don't."

I didn't reply.

"I was just being honest," she reasoned.

"Fine."

"Fine," she repeated back. "Are you being honest with me?"

We stared at each other for a long moment, then I looked away, feeling bruised inside.

Emily turned her skis and started down the slope.

When we arrived at the bottom, the others were relieved to see us.

"What happened?" Dix demanded. "When I didn't pass you on the way down, and you weren't at the bottom—"

"I'm sorry. I didn't mean to make you worry," Emily said. "I took a different route."

Lonnie eyed our snow-covered clothes and started smiling.

If I had learned anything that week, it was how easily appearances could fool. I could guess what she imagined: a romantic kiss in the snow.

We skied for the rest of the morning, Emily selecting harder trails than mine.

"Are you still angry, Quinn?" she asked when we all met for lunch.

I struggled to think of an answer that was honest but would keep me as cool as Quinn. "I wish you'd change your mind," I told her, "but I've got my own prejudices. And I guess you'd probably like to change a few things about the way I think."

"Why?" she asked, pretending to be amazed. "Aren't you perfect?"

"Brat," I said.

Her laughing eyes held mine.

We lined up for lunch at the cafeteria. Feeling starved, I piled onto my tray soup and salad, sandwiches and brownies.

"Got enough to eat, Quinn?" Lonnie teased.

"Harper's been a bad influence on him," Emily observed.

"There's a table. Nab it, Quinn," Dix called from behind us.

"Quinn?" A guy with dark curly hair stood up.

I turned around. "Yes?"

"Quinn Eaton?"

"Yes," I answered warily.

"Told you it was him," a shorter guy said. "Tall. Blond hair. What was it—'eyes as blue as the sky,'" he recalled scornfully.

"Excuse me?" I said.

"Polite, isn't he?" the dark-haired guy remarked, then slammed his fist into my jaw.

I went reeling backward, arms flying—soup, salad, sandwiches, and brownies flying—then slid a few feet on my backside, landing crunched up against a metal trash can. Dix and Harper came running. Security followed. I was dimly aware of people standing up in the cafeteria, someone climbing on a chair trying to see what had happened.

I stared in disbelief at the guy who had slugged me.

"You've fooled around with Sarah," he said in a tense voice. "Then Katie. Now you're hanging around Jen." He ignored the security guard's grip on his arm. "I'm warning you, Eaton. Keep your hands off Jen."

I got up slowly, rubbing the side of my face, and watched them escort the guy out. His pal trailed behind. People at the tables around me stared—surprised, I guess, that a mild-mannered guy wearing chicken noodle soup could break so many girls' hearts. I didn't know what to say, what to do. I got some napkins and cleaned up the mess on the floor as if it was no big deal and cheated boyfriends slugged me all the time.

I was going to kill Quinn, kill him—if I didn't get killed first.

Dix and the others sat down, glancing at one another.

"Guess I need another lunch," I said, and

headed off to stand in line again. A few minutes later Harper came over.

"You okay?" he asked. He looked uncomfortable.

"Harper, I know what you're thinking, and I'm telling you, that guy had me confused with somebody else."

He stood silently for a moment, shifting his weight from foot to foot. "I want to believe you."

"But you can't." I nodded. "Can't say I blame you."

"I mean, I've seen how girls like you. Lonnie, for instance."

So *he* had noticed Lonnie and me. Just when things were straightening out, they were getting all mixed up again. But Lonnie would never forgive me for telling her true feelings to him.

I sighed. "Go eat your lunch before it gets cold."

He nodded and left.

When I arrived at our table, everyone grew silent.

"I don't know what that guy was talking about," I said, sitting down. "It's some kind of mistake." Emily was gazing around the room, looking everywhere but at me. I knew there was no point in saying more than that; only Lonnie would believe me.

That afternoon I skied a lot by myself. Lonnie stuck by me loyally, but she was a much better skier than I, and I didn't want to hold her back. Sometimes we rode to the top together but took different trails down.

Dix stuck like glue to Emily. At one point I caught her staring at me while he talked very quietly. She had a strange look in her eyes. Maybe what he was saying had nothing to do with me. Maybe she was just noticing my attractive purple jaw. But that look in her eyes . . .

It's not true! I wanted to shout. *Whatever he's saying about me, it's not true!*

But I had lost my chance with her. The only way I could win her back now was if I told her I wasn't the infamous Quinn Eaton. And being Jeff Danzig, purchaser of Bell-ringer Specials, I'd lose anyway.

Shadows were growing longer and the snow was shimmering with a pale lilac light. There was time for only one more run. Lonnie and I had just gotten in line when someone came up behind us.

"I've been looking for you," he said in a low voice.

"He's innocent!" Lonnie insisted, wheeling around, ready to punch out the guy.

"Hold on," I told her.

"Quinn," she said.

"Do I know you?" Quinn asked Lonnie.

Lonnie didn't respond. She just stared at him coldly.

Quinn shrugged. "Jeez, that *is* a beauty," he observed, pointing to my jaw. "Does it hurt?"

"Not when it's numb from cold," I replied.

"Would you mind if I took your seat?" Quinn asked Lonnie.

"Mind? *I* sure don't want to sit with you."

He raised one eyebrow. It was an amused expression that worked on a lot of girls. Not Lonnie.

"Emily got a break when *you* didn't show up," she hissed at him, then moved ahead of us.

"I really am sorry about what happened today," Quinn told me. "Do you think you should have your jaw examined by a doctor?"

A chair came down and swooped Lonnie away.

"No, I think you should have *your head* examined. Okay, mine too, for going along with your ridiculous schemes. Cripe, Quinn, can't you find one gorgeous babe and settle down for a while?"

"I could," he agreed as the chair came down behind us. We slid on. "But you're with her."

"What?"

"I couldn't believe it when I saw what Emily looks like now," he said. "Talk about growing up."

I gripped my ski poles.

"I guess you'd like to thank me," he said.

"Oh, yeah. I want to thank you, all right."

"I've been thinking," he continued, "maybe you should leave Deer Hill on the thirty-first."

"New Year's Eve? But I'm supposed to be staying until the dorms open, January second. That was our final agreement."

"It was," Quinn replied, "but I've been thinking things over. My parents are returning late on the thirtieth. I want to make sure they don't suspect anything, so I'm going home the morning of the thirty-first. Just before I do, I'll call you at the

Bellaires' and get the scoop on everything that's happened. You be packed and ready to go. You can come stay with us for the last few days."

"But I agreed to stay at Deer Hill till January second," I said stubbornly, very stubbornly for a guy who claimed he wanted to be away from the place as soon as possible.

"I think you've missed the point," Quinn said. "It wouldn't look good if my parents called the Bellaires to thank them, and I was at home and at the Bellaires' at the same time."

"So stay at Killington. You don't want to miss New Year's Eve," I argued.

"Actually, it's better that I do."

"Oooooh, I get it." I thought that it would be a long way down if I pushed him out of the chair. "Exactly how many girls are expecting to share with you the magic moment of midnight?"

"Three and a maybe. Actually, four and a maybe."

I nodded. "And unfortunately, I'm your only clone."

"I knew you'd understand. One last thing," he said. "Don't blow it with Emily, okay?"

"What do you mean?"

"Don't let that idiot beat you out," he advised.

We were nearing the top.

"Are you referring to Dix?"

"I was watching her with him," he said.

"What does it matter to you?" I demanded.

We leaped simultaneously off the turning chair.

143

"Well, in six months she'll forget what your voice sounds like, and other details," he said.

I pounded my poles into the snow. "I can't believe it!"

"Charm her. Keep her for me."

Now I started waving the poles around like a crazy man. "Keep her for you?" I shouted. "How can I keep her for you when you've fooled around with every girl on the mountain and ruined my—your—whoever's reputation?"

"You'll figure a way," he said confidently. "People have always liked you, Jeff." Then he skied off in a spray of snow.

I shoved off in the opposite direction. Suddenly I felt the mountain falling out from under me. "Holy—"

I have no idea how I made it to the bottom of that double black diamond run still standing.

"Wow," said Lonnie. "I saw you whiz by on the slope."

"Maybe the only way to do it is to let go," I told her.

We walked together toward the lodge.

"Let go of what?" she asked softly.

Twelve

THE BEST PART about being at Killington was that we could ski away from one another. But the next morning we were back at Deer Hill, the five of us in a warm swimming pool surrounded by orchards and orange trees, stuck with one another in the middle of a frozen landscape. Lonnie had wisely headed for the mall to pick up sale stuff for her return to school.

When we emerged from the pool's plush changing rooms, Tracy proved to be the clear winner of the most-amazing-body contest. It was Emily, however, whom I had to tear my eyes from. Every time she looked at me, she looked away. *It's the shiny purple jaw,* I told myself, but I knew it was more than that: As Quinn Eaton, I was a huge letdown. Of course, the lying Jeff Danzig would never restore her faith. Leaving Deer Hill early wasn't a bad idea after all.

That morning Dix showed off his superior diving ability. He was really good at it and could get incredible height off the board. Meanwhile, Tracy told us she had never done anything but jump off the side of a pool. It was clearly just a way to get Harper to hold her waist as she leaned back from the edge of the board and prepared for a back dive, because she turned out to be an expert diver.

The pool building also had a kitchen and lounge area. After swimming, we changed back into our winter clothes and had lunch in the lounge so that we'd be completely dry before going outside again. Lonnie had returned from the mall and brought our meal over in a large picnic hamper. She set a table for us and heated things up in the microwave. I watched Emily, who was watching Harper, who was watching Lonnie.

"Tony said he cleared the pond for you, if you want to skate," she informed us. "The lower one's not completely frozen, but the top one is safe."

"Oh, no, I didn't bring skates," Tracy said. "Do you have a pair I could borrow, Lon? My feet are smaller, but I can wear extra socks. Do you have some thick socks, Harper?"

"There are lots of skates in the barn," Lonnie replied without a hint of resentment, "a range of sizes for guests—where the sleds and hockey sticks are," she reminded Emily and Harper.

"It's awfully cold out," Dix remarked.

"Still, I'd like to go," Harper said, reaching for a

handful of cookies and turning to me. "I'll go if you will, Quinn. You can teach me some hockey moves."

"Sure."

"We'd better start with stick handling and staying on my feet—at the same time," he added, grinning.

"It'll be fun," I told him.

Later, after bundling up back at the house, we all met at the barn. I had brought my own skates. The others sat on trunks, trying on pairs to see which would fit.

Pansy had joined us. She wore a sweater underneath a little dog raincoat. The raincoat was plaid with a hood that tied beneath her chin. It was probably the most ridiculous thing I had ever seen.

"Who's the short skater?" I asked.

Pansy growled. Emily didn't crack a smile—or tell the dog to hush.

"How're we all doing here?" Tony asked, coming into the tack room. "Whoa, nice skates!" he said, noticing mine. "And a nice shade of purple you're wearing there too. Can I see this?"

I nodded and he picked up a skate, slipping off the plastic guard.

"Some edges! I bet these have seen more ice than those cowboy boots have seen horses," he said with a wink.

I grinned. "I do a lot better on my own two legs."

"That's okay," Tony said easily. "Butter likes you all the same. She's been wondering why you haven't come around to pat her nose. I told her I thought you had one too many girlfriends."

I glanced sideways at Emily. She glowered at the skate she was unlacing.

"Am I right?" Tony asked, his eyes crinkling.

"No. I've given up on girls," I said. "I'm tired of being jerked around."

Emily's head bobbed up.

"I've had enough of racing to the wall," I continued, "head on, like we're going to clear it, then suddenly putting on the brakes."

Emily dropped her skate with a clatter. "Tony, where's the sled?" she asked, her voice bristling with irritation.

"Right here. Right here."

A few minutes later we trudged off in our boots. Pansy rode on the sled along with a pile of hockey sticks and skates that we would put on when we reached the ponds.

I was the first one ready. I had never skated on a frozen pond—water doesn't freeze over in Phoenix, and we use an indoor rink at Maplecrest. It was terrific. You had to slide down the pond bank to get to it, the surface was bumpy, and there was a log and branches to skate around, but it was great, with the bright blue sky above and the snowy bowl of land around us. I loved the way our voices rang out and echoed, and the long scrape of my blade across the natural ice.

"Okay, coach," Harper called to me. He was skating toward me, waving two hockey sticks in the air. "I'd give you one, but I think I need them both to keep my balance," he said.

"Clown. Let me have it."

Tracy skated over to us, a stick in one hand, her boots in the other. "To mark the goal," she told us.

I set up the boots. Harper took the puck from his pocket and dropped it on the ice.

Whack!

"Why, look at that thing fly!" Tracy exclaimed as the puck she had just hit zipped across the ice, caromed off the big log, ricocheted off one of Dix's skates, and headed back to us.

She peered down at it. "How exactly are you supposed to hit this little ol' thing?"

"Pretty much like you just did," I said, impressed, "only aimed toward the goal or a teammate. We call it a slap shot."

"A *slap* shot," she repeated, drawing out the word with her southern accent. "I like it. What else?"

"There's a wrist shot," said Harper. "I know what it looks like, but I'm not sure I can do it."

"Try it," I encouraged him.

He skated away from the goal, then turned toward it and took a shot, keeping the stick close to the puck, flicking his wrists. The puck sailed a foot to the left side of the goal.

"Great. Just keep your eyes on the goal," I advised. "You can feel the puck—your stick will tell you where it is."

"So how do we dribble?" Tracy asked, clearing

the puck as if she'd done it a hundred times before. "Is that what you call it in ice hockey?"

"Dribbling or stick handling," Harper told her.

"Am I doing it? How's this?" she asked, carrying the puck up the ice with easy sweeping motions.

"Keep it closer," I instructed. "Someone'll swipe it."

"Try it," she challenged me.

"You ever played this before?" I asked. "Or is this like diving?"

She threw back her head and laughed. "One point for you."

"She's captain of her field hockey team," Dix called over to us. He and Emily were skating at the other end of the long pond.

"She's a natural," I replied.

Tracy passed the puck to Harper, who passed it to me. The three of us wove lazy figure eights on the ice, passing and shooting, taking turns as goaltender.

"Teach me something fancy," Tracy said, her eyes dancing and her cheeks looking like big red apples.

"A flip pass," Harper said.

I nodded, though it wasn't really a fancy move.

"Okay, here's your opponent," I told them, grabbing one of Tracy's boots. "He wants to check you. But you want to pass to the guy behind him."

"Or girl," Tracy inserted.

"Right." I set up her other boot.

Then I backed up and started skating toward the

first boot. Just before I reached it, I tilted my blade away from the puck and scooped the puck onto the blade's heel, lifting it. With a flick of my wrists, I flipped the puck neatly over the boot.

"Cool," she said.

"Okay, now I'm the enemy," I told them.

Tracy and Harper practiced the pass over and over. They laughed and teased each other. Dix joined us as I was demonstrating the backhand flip.

"Good move!" I said when Dix took a turn. He glanced at me, his mouth twisting up on one side.

"I mean it," I added, surprised by the sardonic look.

"I've played before," he replied coolly.

"Oh. Well, good." A voice inside me said, *Great. Take him on.* He might be familiar with the game, but from the way he moved, I knew I could wipe him off the ice.

"Why don't we play some two-on-two?" Harper suggested.

Dix shook his head. "Don't take this the wrong way, Harper, but you'd kill yourself. Before you play, you've got to be really sure on your skates."

"You'll do fine," I contradicted him, hoping to keep up Harper's newfound confidence. "You've got a good wrist shot. We'll be a team, you and I. Tullys bring it in first."

Harper looked over at Tracy, smiling a little.

"Stay with her," I directed him. "Watch the puck, watch her stick. Don't let those hips fake you out."

Tracy laughed. "These hips have had a lot of practice."

"All right," Dix said, realizing the rest of us would play without him, "if you insist. How many points are we playing to?"

"Do we have to keep score?" Harper responded.

"It's a game; what do you think?" Dix replied.

"I think it's just a game," I said. "But if you want to keep score, Dix, we will."

His eyes flashed. That was what he liked—competition. "We'll play to a combined fifteen," he said. "Aren't you going to stay and watch, Emily?"

Of course she's not, I thought bitterly. *Why would she stay around and watch my one chance to shine?*

She had already taken off her skates. "I'll be back," she called to him. "I'm going to take Pansy for a walk."

Just as well, I told myself. Now that she was gone, I could forget hotdogging and concentrate on helping Harper look good—and maybe earn the small satisfaction of landing Dix on his rump once or twice.

We started playing. I moved in aggressively on Dix but didn't bodycheck. A poke check with my stick sent the puck skittering away from him. Both of us chased it, flying down the ice elbow to elbow. It rebounded off a branch embedded in the ice, skidding to Dix's side. He cradled it, then headed for the goal. Out of the corner of my eye I saw

Tracy fake around Harper. She skated toward the slot, perfectly positioned. Dix had to see her too.

But he didn't pass. I used a hook check. Then, seeing that Tracy had again put herself in perfect position, I let him retrieve the puck. He still didn't pass.

Want to beat a guy? Team him up with his sister. Dix didn't want to pass to her for anything.

I snatched the puck and sent it out to Harper. As soon as I was free of Dix, Harper relayed it back to me. His pass was off target. I raced to catch up with the sailing puck.

Dix raced beside me, chopping at the ice with his skates.

I got there first. When I spun around, he body-checked me, slamming me with his hips. I decked him and moved toward the goal.

He caught me with an illegal hook, banging me with his stick.

"Hey," I shouted, "we're not wearing equipment!"

"Too rough?" he challenged.

"Nope."

I let him get ahead of me, knowing he couldn't resist bumping me again, and guessing he'd broadcast his move. Just as I thought: I saw the body check coming and stepped out of the way. With nothing to throw his weight against, Dix spun around. While he tried to recover, I scooted past him, skating close to Tracy, drawing her out.

Harper looked left and right, as if he didn't

know which way to skate. I kept Tracy dancing around me. "In the slot, Harper!"

"Oh!"

My backhand flip popped the puck over Tracy's blade. Harper took it in for the goal.

"Yes!" I said.

He glowed.

"Revenge!" cried Tracy, diving in to clear the puck. But whether the revenge was against us or Dix, I couldn't tell. Because Tracy wouldn't pass to her brother. Unlike him, however, she was able to score.

The score climbed to 6–1. Tracy's second goal was scored on a follow-up shot after Dix banged the puck off the boot.

"Nice one!" I hollered.

When Dix refused to give her a high five, Harper and I held out our hands.

Dix was getting steamed. Good. The hotter he got, the easier he was to play around.

"Drop pass. Behind me, Harp," I called.

I left the puck dead on the ice, then set a screen, blocking out Tracy. Harper skated it in for a goal.

"Yo!" shouted Harper, his face showing his own disbelief that he had done it again.

The score went to 7–3. 8–4. 9–4. Tracy fought like a cat.

Harper was looking like a hero. It was fun to set him up. But Dix was getting to be a drag, hacking away at me. I'd had enough. Hearing his skates behind me, I made a sudden pass. Harper's stick magically found the puck and slipped it right between the boots.

"Eleven-four! That's it!"

Harper and I skated toward each other with our hockey sticks raised in triumph. We collided and fell down.

Tracy skated over and fell down with us, laughing.

"I'm not sure I'd want to take you on one-on-one," I told her. I admired her spirit as well as her skill.

"Yeah? Well, you've got yourself a match. But first give me a time-out." She turned to Harper. "You did great!" she said. "Hey, Dix."

He was keeping his distance—sulking, I thought.

"Come here," his sister coaxed.

"Something's wrong," he said.

"Oh, come on, Dixie—"

"Something's wrong!"

The next moment we heard Emily shouting. She was calling Pansy and her voice sounded panicky.

We scrambled to our feet.

"Em!" Harper yelled at her when he saw what was going on. "Don't!"

Pansy had ventured onto the lower, snow-covered pond. Emily was trying to get her, edging out on the dangerously thin layer of ice.

We raced to the other end of our ice, then stumbled onto the bank, running clumsily in our skates to the lower pond. Emily was already ten feet from its bank and moving slowly, steadily toward the dog.

"Emily, come back!" Harper demanded.

"Do what we say!" Tracy shouted.

"It's just a dog," Dix reasoned with her.

A stupid dog, I thought, but to Emily she wasn't—Pansy was a loyal friend who cuddled close to her when Emily needed comfort.

The dog paced nervously on the ice, barking a little, walking toward the area where the frozen surface turned lead gray. A few inches beyond, the edge of the ice was washed by dark water.

"Come on, Pan," Emily called gently. Her voice shook. "Come on, girl, please."

"Emily, come back," Harper pleaded. "You're too heavy for the ice. You'll both go in."

I bent down over my skates, my fingers ripping at the laces. I got one loose.

"Somebody go for help," Dix said.

"I'm fastest," Tracy replied, and began to undo her skates.

"Pansy, come here. Now!" Emily's voice was sharp with fear.

"How deep is it?" I asked. If I approached from the other side, I'd have to wade out about fifteen feet to reach the dog.

"You'll freeze," said Harper.

"How deep?"

"In the center, eight feet, maybe nine," he said. "Less here."

I started in.

Tracy stopped to stare at me. "Keep going," I told her as I waded in farther. "Get help. Go!"

Then the intense, unbelievable cold wrapped it-self around me. It burrowed into my bones. My skin felt burned where the water hemmed my legs. For a moment I didn't move, stunned by the cold. I'd have to work fast if I was going to make it.

"Emily, get back. Get back now."

She looked at me in bewilderment, then step by step moved back toward the bank.

I moved forward as fast as I could, but it felt unbearably slow. The water was muddy black, a cold, thick pudding. I felt as though I were in a slow-motion dream.

Pansy started to bark repeatedly. I wondered if she could swim in the cold water. The raincoat would make it more difficult.

"Stay, girl," I said. "Stay."

A piece of ice went soft beneath the dog's feet and she leaped back.

"Good. Keep going, go back to Em."

But she didn't. She was afraid and confused. She began to whimper.

The solid cold crept up past my waist. Up to my chest. I gritted my teeth. Almost there.

Suddenly the ice gave way. Pansy went sliding down, past my hand.

I went down after her, groping in the freezing darkness.

Let me find her, let me find her, I prayed. *Please!*

My hand caught something. It was so cold—it could have been a submerged branch, a rock, a dog.

157

I pulled it up swiftly. Pansy was panicked and gagging. I gripped her tightly against me and started back to shore. My legs were so numb, I couldn't feel the pond bottom and stumbled over rocks. I pushed forward again, then slid on something and went down to my knees. The cold absorbed my energy. I couldn't get up. Too tired. The water was freezing on my face, freezing in my ears.

The others reached out for me and yanked me up the bank.

"P-Put her under your jacket," I stammered, handing Pansy to Emily.

Dix and Harper had their sweaters off and were drying my head and wrapping their jackets around me.

"We have to get him back," Dix said. "We have to get him warm."

"Come on. Fast as you can, Quinn," Harper said. "Get his other side, Dix."

"How about the sled?" Dix asked.

"It won't be much faster, and he might stay warmer if he uses his legs," Harper reasoned.

I was being talked about, rather than to, which made me feel weird. They just about lifted me off the ground, dragging me up the hill toward the house.

"Emily, you okay?" Harper asked over his shoulder.

"Okay," she called back. "There's the Jeep. Tony!"

It came bouncing over the hill. A minute later,

there was a lot of excited talking and some shoving. I got stuffed in like groceries.

"I'll tell you, Emmy," I heard Tony say as he turned the Jeep around, "this one sure keeps things exciting."

"Drive, Tony," she said, her voice quivering.

He drove fast.

I shut my eyes and dreamed about desert heat.

Thirteen

WHAT HAPPENED AFTER that was all a blur. I remember Lonnie, Lonnie's parents, and Gamby standing at the door of the main house. Emily must have handed the dog to someone, for I suddenly felt her arms tight around me.

That didn't last long. Tony, Dix, and Harper dragged me off to a hot shower. "Easy now, easy," Tony said. "Warm him up slowly."

What they called "lukewarm water" felt like fire on my frozen skin.

Next thing I remember was the weight of blankets on top of me. As soon as I had emerged from the warm shower, the cold had seeped back into my body. Now Mrs. Dove and Emily were trying to get me to sip hot soup. I felt very tired. Slowly the warmth of the soup spread through me, and with it, a heavy sleep.

I must have slept several hours. I awoke sweat-

160

ing. Throwing off the blankets, I rose and went to the bedroom window. It was twilight and the lights in the courtyard twinkled. Window candles were being lit room by room in the main house.

I lit my own candles as well as a small bedside lamp. Just after I finished dressing, someone knocked on my door. Hoping that it was Emily, I opened it quickly.

"Mr. Bellaire!"

"Hello, Quinn. May I?" he asked politely.

"Uh, sure." I stepped back to let him in.

He was dressed in a tux—heading out for another holiday party, I guessed. When he entered the room he glanced around, then walked over to the window to look out, turning his head to the left, gazing at the main house. "Pretty. They've done a nice job," he remarked, as if he were seeing someone else's home. Then he turned around and studied me.

"How are you feeling?"

"Fine. Fine, sir."

He nodded. "Good."

"Uh, how's Pansy?" I asked.

"She survived. The dumb ones always do. Quinn," he said, "we'll have no more heroics in this house, is that understood?"

"Yes," I replied, "but you had better tell your daughter too. She was walking ten feet out on very thin ice."

He smiled and grimaced at the same time. "So I

161

hear. Emily and that dog are much too attached to each other. It's idiotic."

Ever wonder why Emily needs so much affection from a pet? I thought, but didn't say it.

"Of course," he said, "Mrs. Bellaire and I are very appreciative of your effort."

"No problem," I said, shrugging it off.

"Where shall I put this?" he asked.

He had drawn something out of his pocket. I realized suddenly that it was a check. They were paying me for the rescue.

"Thanks, but I don't want it, sir."

"I think every young man wants a little spending money," he said knowingly.

"Sure, but not for this. I did what I did because I care about Emily."

"It's a thousand dollars," he persisted.

"That's how much you think she's worth?"

"So you want more," he replied.

"I don't want it at all. Take it back."

Mr. Bellaire cocked his head. I think it actually annoyed him that I would refuse his money. Apparently the rule was that Senator Tully couldn't ask for it, but I couldn't refuse it. "Think again," he said quietly, placing it on my dresser.

What Mr. Bellaire liked more than money, I realized, was control.

He pulled out his checkbook. "I'll add another thousand. In effect, you rescued both Emily and the dog."

"If you want to show your appreciation," I said,

162

"give Emily a hug. Let her know you think she's terrific."

The man looked at me as if I had just touched down from Mars. Truth was, I felt about as strange as an alien. Two thousand dollars—what I could do with it! But I knew I'd never spend it. It cheapened everything, including Emily and *my* idiotic attachment to her. Mr. Bellaire wrote the check, signed it, and tore it from his book. What I could buy with two thousand dollars!

"Keep it," I said, thrusting the first check into his hand with the new one. "I don't want your money."

He looked at me steadily. Then he made a neat tear down the middle of the checks and dropped them in my wastebasket, watching me for a reaction. "You know," he said at last, "you're nothing like your father."

He turned and left.

As soon as the door closed, I retrieved the checks and ripped them into shreds—before I thought too much about getting out the tape.

I ran into Emily in the gallery that connected the guest wing with the house. For a moment neither of us said anything.

While getting dressed, I had thought of all kinds of little jokes about the incident at the pond, hoping to make it seem like no big deal. But it was a big deal to me—I don't know what scared me more, the memory of that deathlike cold overtaking me or the realization of what I'd do for Emily. Looking at her now, I struggled to remember one funny line.

If she had planned a little speech—you know, *Thanks for saving my darling dog, you are so brave and kind*—she had forgotten it too. We just stared at each other.

"Say something," I told her. "One of us has to break the ice."

She winced. Bad joke.

"You idiot! You jerk!"

"You're welcome," I said, taken aback. *And here I thought I'd get a few words of thanks!*

"You crazy fool!"

"Please," I said, "you'll give me a big head."

"I don't understand, I don't understand," she repeated, grabbing on to my sweater, her hand in a tight fist.

"Good. I was beginning to think I was the only one."

"Why did you do such a thing? How could you be so stupid?"

I was getting angry, then I noticed her eyes were wet at the corners. She blinked them hard.

"Because I love—Pansy. Isn't it obvious?"

"Do you know how dangerous it was?" Both of her hands were yanking on my sweater. "Do you realize what could have happened?"

"Sure. Pansy could have passed on to little-doggy heaven," I said. "We would have had a funeral and invited all her shaggy friends. Does she have any?"

"You jerk," Emily sobbed, and put her face against my sweater, though she held the rest of herself away from me.

"Give it up," I said softly. "Give it up, Em." I pulled her close.

Her arms went around me. I held her tight, lowering my face against her face. She was crying hard.

"It's okay, Emily. Everything's all right."

"I was so scared," she said. "If something had happened to you . . ."

I could feel her shaking. "Nothing did," I replied, smoothing her hair with my hand.

She let me hold her for a long time.

"You make me all mixed up," she said.

I rubbed her back in slow circles, the way my mom used to when I was a little boy.

She suddenly pulled back. Her green eyes were shining, her lashes dark and wet. "You know, don't you, I've got it bad for you? I never meant to fall for you," she went on. "Jeez, I can't believe I said that. Don't take it the wrong way—though I guess there is only one way you can take it. It sounds like a lousy thing to say, but . . ."

"I didn't mean to fall for you either," I told her.

She laid her head against me. "Now what do we do?"

"Don't know." I just wanted to hold her. And hold her. "I suppose you could go find Dix and flirt a little. And I could pack up and leave early." As Quinn had asked me to, I thought.

"Dix is out. He went into town for dinner with Tracy and Harper."

"Did he?"

"And Lonnie's gone to visit a friend who's having a party. While you were sleeping, she and I talked a lot about Harp. She really needed to get away tonight."

"I wish it were different for her."

"Me too." She was silent for a moment. "Mum and Dad are out for the evening. Mr. Dove drove them. Gamby's gone home."

She reached up and touched my face gently. It would be impossible for me to leave early.

"Mrs. Dove has left some dinner for us," she went on.

"We're alone?"

"Almost," she said, smiling and glancing out of the corner of her eye.

Pansy, looking fluffed up, sat on a bench in the gallery, watching us.

"I didn't hear her come in," I said. "I mean I didn't hear her growl."

Emily smiled and looked up at me. The heat and cold, the waves of hope and fear I'd felt during the rescue, were nothing compared to what swept through me now.

"Emily, I—I love—"

"Yes?"

"Pansy."

She blinked.

"I guess I mentioned that before," I said.

166

She laughed. "You did." Then she pulled my head down. Her lips were an inch from mine. A half inch. They met. The kiss was long and tender. I could hardly believe it was Emily trembling in my arms.

"Em," I whispered.

"Stay," she said, holding me tight. "Stay as long as you can."

I didn't want to let go of her. I was afraid I'd wake up and find this was a dream. She rested against me for a long time.

"You must be getting hungry," she said after a while.

"No. Yes. My stomach's hungry. My arms don't want to move."

"Come on," she said, laughing. She led me by the hand. "Is a table for two in the kitchen okay with you?"

I smiled. "The kitchen's my favorite room here."

"Thought so."

When we passed through the dining room she picked up a large candelabra and handed it to me, then carried another herself. "We'll eat by candlelight," she said as we entered the kitchen.

We sure did. While the microwave beeped and I stirred and spooned out the dinners Mrs. Dove had left behind, Emily gathered candlesticks. We sat down to the glow of twenty-eight candles, sixteen in the two candelabra, and twelve others in an assortment of holders placed on our table, and the stove, the countertops, the window ledges.

The room turned a warm gold and Emily's face itself was alight. We poked at our food and gazed at each other. Maybe it was a good thing no one was around right then, while we drank each other up. Since that first afternoon tea with her I had been trying to be so cool; now I was making up for lost time, just staring.

"Aren't you hungry?" she asked.

"Oh, yeah, I am. How about you?" She had eaten no more than a roll.

"I hate peas," she said.

"I'm not crazy about acorn squash."

"Trade?"

We ate off each other's plates, our arms brushing, tingling with each touch.

"Peas are squishy," she said. "And dented, like some little creature's been walking on them."

"You know, when I was four years old, I thought that Jesus and his mother slept in them."

"What?"

"In the Christmas carol 'Silent Night,'" I explained, "the last line—'Sleep in heavenly peas.'"

Emily burst out laughing. "Peace! You must have been a very bright preschooler."

"Top of my class in cookie breaks."

"I love your eyes," she said. "I could drown in them."

I looked at her, surprised, and she clapped her hand over her mouth, embarrassed.

I started to laugh.

"Why are you laughing?"

"Why are you holding your hand over your mouth?" I asked, pulling it away.

"Because it seemed like a stupid thing to say while we're talking about peas and cookie breaks."

I shook my head. "You said something you were thinking, something that makes me feel great. How is that stupid?"

She looked down at her plate.

"Emily?"

She wouldn't look up.

"Emily, you don't have to fake it with me, okay? Just say what's on your mind."

She nodded, still staring at her plate. "Being with you, it feels really hard and really easy at the same time," she said. "It feels as if I can say anything to you, but then I start to think, what if I say the wrong thing? Know what I mean?"

"Yeah. Oh, yeah."

She looked up at me, biting her lip, then smiled and reached for my hand. "Stay as long as you can," she said for the second time.

Like I could do anything else.

Fourteen

WHEN THE OTHERS returned that evening, Emily and I were sitting together in an oversized armchair watching a video. Harper talked about their dinner, shifting his weight from foot to foot, staring at the spot where my hand rested on Emily's. Dix asked if I had done anything else heroic that evening, then made a quick exit. Only Tracy seemed at ease, sitting down with us to watch the end of the movie.

Tuesday morning, as I reached the door of the breakfast room, I heard funny puppy yips. Pansy trotted toward me—too slowly for a dog preparing to leap for my jugular. She sat down and wagged her tail.

"Hi," I said without enthusiasm.

She flopped down on my foot, her little tail beating against the floor.

"Okay, now how am I supposed to walk?"

"You're not," Emily answered, coming in from the kitchen. "She wants you to pet her."

Pansy rolled over on her back, and when I didn't do anything, she waved her front paws in the air.

"She's just conning me," I said. "When I reach down, she'll take my hand off."

"Still feeling jerked around by girls?" Emily teased. She stepped close to me and kissed me on the mouth.

"Guess not," I said, swiping a second delicious kiss. Then I stooped down to rub Pansy's belly. "I liked you better the other way," I whispered to the dog.

Harper and Dix entered the breakfast room, with Tracy following.

"After that dinner last night, I just can't eat another thing," Tracy told us.

"I'm starved," said Harper.

"I'm coming," said Mrs. Dove, pushing through the door, carrying a tray of sliced fruit. Gamby followed behind with a pot of coffee and the usual selection of newspapers tucked under her arm.

"Is Lonnie up yet?" Harper asked.

"I don't know, dear," Dovey replied. "She stayed at a friend's last night. Any special requests for juice?"

"Which friend?" Harper asked.

"Julie. Orange? Cranberry? Apple?" Mrs. Dove went on. "Robert will pick up more grapefruit today."

"And three dozen candles," Gamby muttered,

arranging things on the sideboard. "The missus likes her candles fresh. We need three dozen," she said.

"Actually, Gamby, it was only twenty-six," Emily told her, smiling.

"And Robert will be very glad to fetch them," Dovey said soothingly.

While she took juice orders, Emily and Tracy discussed the previous night's movie. Pansy sat next to my chair and looked up at me lovingly. Dix read the newspaper, *The Wall Street Journal*—he was checking stock prices! He folded the paper into neat quarters, the way I had seen businessmen do on an airplane. I wondered if Emily would notice him and wish that the guy she liked to kiss would act more sophisticated.

"So who do you want to watch in the bowl games this year?" I asked Harper.

"Florida State. I always watch Florida State."

Right now, however, he was watching the back driveway that looped around the lawn and patio. We could see it through the double doors of the breakfast room. A moment later, I saw what he was waiting for.

A dark green Volvo pulled up and Lonnie got out. So did the driver—a tall, very good-looking guy. Lonnie waved him back into the car. The guy looked disappointed, and he watched Lonnie as she scurried across the snow-covered patio. She must have entered the kitchen door. Her escort slowly, reluctantly, got back into his car, then backed down the driveway. Harper glowered at his fruit cup.

He looked up sharply when Mrs. Dove entered with the juice tray. Gamby followed with scrambled eggs and toast. The oven timer went off and both women glanced toward the kitchen. Two minutes later, Lonnie came in, still wearing her coat, carrying a basket of hot muffins.

"Thank you, love," her mother said.

"How was your sleepover?" Harper asked Lonnie.

"Terrific," she replied. Her cheeks were still pink from the cold.

"Hey, Lon," Emily said softly. That's all she said. Lonnie looked first at Emily and then at me, then smiled a wide and beautiful smile. It's one of those mysterious things about girls, the way they can communicate with almost no words. Somehow Lonnie now knew that Emily and I were together.

"How's Julie?" Harper asked.

"Fine. She had a party," Lonnie told him. "I got to see a lot of my old friends."

"That didn't look like Julie," Harper remarked.

Lonnie had begun serving the muffins with a pair of tongs. She stopped and frowned.

"The guy in the Volvo," Harper prompted.

Lonnie dropped the muffin from high up, letting it plop on his plate. "You mean Julie's cousin."

"I guess he was staying with her family for the holidays," Harper persisted nosily.

"No."

He waited for Lonnie to say more.

173

She let her answer hang in the air while she worked her way around the table. "Sam came over this morning to help us clean up," she told Harper as she headed back to the kitchen.

Gamby was holding the door for her. "Before I forget, Lonnie, Tim called to say he'd pick you up a half hour earlier tonight."

I looked at Gamby in surprise. The housekeeper had spoken in an obvious stage whisper; she must have wanted Harper to hear her.

"Thanks."

The door swung closed behind them.

"Dix, there's food on the table," his sister told him. "Put down that newspaper and let us see your face."

Dix placed the paper on the table. We saw his face as he read and chewed.

"There are a lot of grumpy boys around here this morning," Tracy remarked.

"Not me," I told her, and chowed down.

When we were almost finished, Mrs. Dove came in. "Miss Emily, your mum wants to see you as soon as you're done here," she said. "It's about preparations for tomorrow's New Year's Eve gathering."

Emily nodded. "I'm finished now." She passed her hand lightly over mine. "Maybe we can go sledding today. Catch you later, okay?"

Pansy followed Emily to the door, gave me one long, tender doggy look—cripe!—then disappeared.

"I guess I'll use the time to do something

about these awful nails," Tracy said, holding up her hands. "They grow like mad. What color do you think I should start the New Year with? Harper?"

"I don't know."

"I'll give you a choice," she said. "Cloud Pink. Silver Bell. Blue Dazzle. Or Lime Ice."

"Whatever," he said unenthusiastically.

Her lips began to form a pout. But she quickly put a smile on her face and smacked her hands down on the table. "Well, then, it's Lime Ice—at least on one hand."

She left to do creative things to her fingers. Her brother trailed her out of the room without saying a word.

When Harper and I were alone, I turned to him. "You don't seem too hungry."

"What? Oh." He dutifully attacked the eggs with his fork and lifted them to his mouth.

"How are you getting along with Tracy?" I asked.

"She's okay."

"Just okay?" I baited.

"She's nice. I guess."

I played with my silverware. "I think she really likes you."

He shrugged. "She knows how to flatter a guy, how to make you feel good," he replied. "She also knows how to get what she wants, how to handle things—how to handle me, if you know what I mean."

I was surprised that Harper saw her so clearly.

"You interested in somebody else?" I ventured.

He looked up at me, his eyes round. "Like who?"

"Well—"

The door to the kitchen swung open. Harper and I both turned around.

"Oh, sorry," Lonnie said. "I thought you were finished."

"I am," Harper replied, shoving back his chair.

"Both of us are," I said. "We'll help you clear."

Harper started stacking plates. "Lonnie," he said, "isn't Tim the guy you dated last year?"

"Yes."

"And isn't he the one that was running around with a lot of girls?"

She gathered up spoons. "So?"

"Isn't he the one who's kind of fast?" Harper persisted.

"What does it matter to you?" she asked, clanking the silverware together. She started collecting cups and saucers.

"It doesn't, of course. But, well, I think maybe you should be careful," he said.

She stared at him, stared until he met her eyes.

"I'm just giving you a little . . . brotherly advice," he explained.

"You're not my brother, Harper."

"I know that," he said humbly.

"And I've got a father."

"I know."

"Then maybe you know it's time to butt out!"

He looked stung. "I just want you to be happy, Lon," he insisted. "You've never dated any one guy for too long and—"

"Like you've had a special girl?" she exploded.

"That's different," he replied.

Her eyes flashed. I quickly stuck out a hand to steady her teetering stack of dishes. "You chauvinist!" she charged him.

"What I mean is that I've never been good at dating, so naturally I wouldn't," Harper said patiently.

She softened a little.

"And you could have whatever guy you wanted," he told her. "I want you to get somebody worthy of you."

She looked as if she was going to cry.

"I keep saying the wrong thing, don't I?" he added miserably.

"Harper," she said softly, "I need to see a lot of people right now."

"Why?"

Tell him the truth, Lonnie, I thought. *Tell him how you feel.*

She swallowed hard. "I, uh, I've fallen for someone."

"You have?" I think he stopped breathing. "You mean . . . *really* fallen?"

"Yeah. For someone who can't be mine. And it's making me feel bad."

I saw Harper's shoulders relax. He was glad the "other guy" couldn't be hers. But then he looked unhappy for her. "I'm sorry," he said. "I'm sorry, Lon."

"Me too," she replied, and laughed. "Anyway, it helps to get out and see different people. Understand?"

He nodded solemnly. We finished clearing the table, and Lonnie carried the dishes into the kitchen.

"I guess I'd better see if Mum needs my help," Harper told me, but his mind was far from what he was saying. He walked straight into the sideboard, looked at the piece of furniture in amazement, then bungled his way out the door.

I began to roll up the long tablecloth, careful to keep the crumbs inside.

Lonnie came out of the kitchen again. "I'll take care of that."

"You get the other side," I replied. "How are you doing, Lon?"

"Fine. Great." We met at the middle. "*Awful!*" she said, and burst into tears.

I put my hands on her shoulders, then around her shoulders, then both arms around her. She had pent up an ocean of tears since arriving home for Christmas. She cried and cried. I patted her back a lot.

"You should tell him," I said when her sobs had subsided.

"I can't." She began to hiccough.

I rubbed her back—sort of like I had rubbed Emily's. I was becoming a pro at this. Unfortunately, neither of us heard the footsteps headed toward the breakfast room.

"Can you tell him in writing?" I asked.

"No," she said, her voice quivering.

"Okay, okay," I soothed. "What if I tell Harper?"

Then we both looked up, aware of someone standing in the doorway. Harper.

His cheeks went scarlet. He turned and hurried away.

"Oh, cripe," I muttered.

Lonnie sagged against me.

"I'd better go explain, Lon."

"No!" she said quickly.

"Lonnie, we've got to get this cleared up. Harper probably thinks I'm the one you've fallen for and we don't know how to tell him—or Emily."

She shook her head. "Emily knows what's going on. That's all that counts."

"But—"

"Things are okay for you," she said. "Just let it be."

"But—"

"Please! I've talked to my parents. They need me to help them get ready for New Year's Eve. After that, I'm out of here."

I shook my head.

"It's my choice, Jeff. It's my life, not yours. Don't say anything. Promise?"

"I think you're making a mistake," I told her, then sighed. "Promise."

Fifteen

TONY HAD LEANED a row of sleds against the barn. Dix joined the rest of us a few minutes late and was acting like his old self, telling us about the wonderful snowmobiles the Tullys owned. Then the five of us set off on a short hike to the sledding hill.

"Tracy," Dix said, "remember the Christmas we spent in the Austrian Alps, when we went tobogganing at midnight?"

"Under a full moon," she replied.

"What about the Christmas in southern France?" Dix asked. "Do you remember New Year's Eve on the Riviera?"

"The fireworks over the water," Tracy recalled. Her spiky blond hair looked like feathers around her earmuffs. She was hauling two sleds, unable to decide which one she wanted to use.

Harper walked beside her, but in another world, so

he didn't think to help with the extra sled. I was dragging along Pansy, who had chosen to hitch a ride on my Flexible Flyer. Today she was wearing a blue sweater with a snowflake pattern. I imagined a little closet in Emily's room, full of miniature sweaters and coats, collars and bows.

"What are you thinking?" Emily asked, seeing me smile.

"That I want to kiss you," I said softly.

She squeezed my hand.

Harper trudged on silently.

"I really enjoyed England," Dix continued the travelogue. "The service at the abbey, singing the carols. The castle was a little chilly, though."

I wondered how Dix would enjoy Bing Crosby on my father's boom box at the Desert Shade Trailer Park.

Dix turned to me. "Where have you spent your holidays, Quinn?"

"At home."

"So this is quite a change for you," he observed.

"You could say that."

"When are your parents due back?" he asked.

Why does he want to know? I wondered. "Let's see. What's today—the thirtieth? Sometime today," I replied as casually as possible.

We had finally reached the top of the hill. It dropped forty feet or so, then rose gradually and made a second long drop, ending in a path that led into the woods. I turned to Emily and Harper. "This is great!"

Harper still hadn't spoken a word.

"So, Em," Dix said, "does everyone in the house have to go to tea tomorrow?"

I didn't like him calling her Em. He didn't know her well enough, I thought—as if I had known her longer.

"Yes. Mum always makes us have high tea with her on New Year's Eve."

"Fun," he said, as though he really thought it was. "What happens after that?"

"About seven o'clock a few party guests arrive, whoever's staying overnight. The others come after nine."

"The same group every year?" he wanted to know.

I wondered what was behind all these questions.

"Oh, no," Emily told him. "Different people— whoever's around. There are always surprises."

"Really." He ran his gloved hand along the runner of his sled, looking very thoughtful.

"You want to go first?" I asked him.

"If you'd like me to, Quinn."

Dix positioned himself for a running start and pulled it off as smoothly as one of his dives. I wished he'd get lost in the woods below. Maybe I was just imagining the sly look in his eyes, but his inquiries about my "parents" and the events slated for tomorrow were making me nervous.

Emily touched my hand. "Can I ride with you?" she asked.

I smiled. "I was hoping."

Giggling like little kids, we climbed on the sled. She sat up front on the old Flyer, and I sat behind, wrapping my legs around hers, resting my feet on the crossbar.

"I'll hold on to the sled, you hold on to me," she said.

"Okay. Ready."

"By the way, how much experience do you have steering one of these?"

"Almost none," I replied.

"That's what I thought. Give us a shove, Harper," she called to her brother.

He gave us a huge one. We flew down the hill. *Bump! Thump!* The sled leaped in the air, then hit the ground again.

"Yow!"

"Ride 'em, cowboy!" I shouted.

We kept on going, passing Dix, who was climbing up the hill, rounding the top of the second hill, slowing, slowing, then picking up speed again, down, down, faster and faster.

Emily's hair flew out of her cap like shiny ribbons. I could hear her, feel her laughing in my arms.

"To the right!" she shouted.

I jammed my foot hard against the crossbar and we veered sharply. For a moment we were on the path through the woods, then the sled ran off it and among the trees. We zigzagged crazily as I tried to avoid stumps and branches. Sun flashed through. We were in a small clearing.

"Let go!" I shouted, pulling Emily off the sled with me just before we crashed into a pine.

She tumbled on top of me, laughing and pounding my chest. "You sled worse than you ride."

"I sled fine. It was the navigator who screwed up," I said, giving her a little push.

She jumped back on top of me. "You could have killed us both."

"Next time, tell me five feet *before* rather than five feet *after* we've passed the turning point."

We wrestled in the snow, rolling over and over, laughing. Then she grew very still. I became still too. Looking at her made me breathless. We kissed, then lay back in the snow.

"I can't believe how happy I am," Emily said, closing her eyes.

The sky was brilliant blue, like the sky in Arizona. The warm sun, the reflection of it off the bright snow, and the heat inside me made me think of home, the desert. I wished more than anything that I could show it to her.

"What a look on your face," Emily said, pulling herself up on one elbow, touching my lips gently. "What a sad smile! What are you thinking about?"

"Arizona."

She cocked her head. "What about it?"

"Ever been there?"

"No," she said quietly. "Have you?"

I nodded.

"Tell me what it's like."

"Well . . . the desert air is very clear," I said. "I

184

feel so alive when I'm out walking. Everything shimmers. The cholla, its silvery needles catching the light. The big saguaros, when the sun drops gold behind them. There's life all around you. Little ground squirrels. Quail. Javelinas, if you're lucky enough to see them. Snakes, of course."

"Of course. You sound as if you wish you were there."

"I wish I could take you there."

Her smile made me ache. I could never take her, not unless I wanted to spend big bucks and rent a place at some posh golf resort. Our bungalow was smaller than the servants' quarters where the Doves lived.

I tried to imagine Emily in my own environment. I could see my mother at their first meeting, dressed up in her rodeo queen outfit, setting out burritos on television trays. It was a stupid wish— I'd never take Emily home.

"You keep sighing," she said, snuggling next to me.

I had to tell her the truth, but I didn't know where to begin.

"Emily, I keep falling for you. I think I feel as much as I could ever feel about someone, and then I feel even more."

"Do you," she said, smiling at me.

"I can't stop thinking about you. All I want is to be with you. I'd do *anything* to be with you—it's not a good thing."

"It's a wonderful thing!"

"Listen to me," I pleaded, catching her face in my

185

hands. "There's a lot you don't know about me."

"You mean about the other girls in your life?"

"What? Oh, that," I said, remembering the incident at the ski lodge.

"Do you want me to forgive you?" she asked.

I sat up. *Just blurt it out,* I told myself, but I hesitated.

"I see. You don't want forgiveness," she said, sitting up with me. "You're proud of yourself."

"Anything but," I replied unhappily.

"You know what I think?"

I shook my head.

"I think there's really only one other girl that counts."

"What? No. There's no other girl but you."

She raised a dark eyebrow. "No one else that you want to be with this holiday?"

"I just told you," I said.

"I don't believe you," she replied.

I was puzzled. Maybe Harper had told her what he'd witnessed in the dining room.

"Emily, if you're still thinking Lonnie and I have something going—that was just bad timing. Harper had been asking Lonnie about the guys she was seeing. She got upset. Later, when he walked in, I was comforting her. She's really in love with him," I said. "And he is with her, I can see it." It was a relief to be talking about them rather than me. "We should do something to help them."

"We should stay out of it," Emily answered.

"But they need each other," I insisted. "They're right for each other."

"That's not how our parents would see it," she said, and shook the snow off her hat.

"*Your* parents," I corrected her.

"The Doves too!" she exclaimed angrily. "Don't you get it?"

"Oh, I get it all right."

"You think we're all snots," she said quickly.

"I didn't say that."

"It's written all over your face."

I stood up.

"Listen," she said, grabbing my hand, "I want to see Lonnie and Harper together as much as you do, probably more. But I know what the reaction will be. And then there will be a lot of hurt, even more than there is now, once our parents make sure that they are kept apart."

It's not fair, I wanted to shout. But it was how it was—and it was how it would be for her and me. If only she knew I was arguing for the two of us as much as for them.

We made a lot of sled runs that afternoon, but none of them was like that first one. Emily and I both acted as if everything was fine, but the next time I rode with my arms around her, she did not lean back against me.

The temperature climbed throughout the afternoon and the snow was beginning to melt. By the time we arrived back from sledding, all of us were soaked and in lousy moods. Except Dix—he was annoyingly cheerful.

Supper was sent to each of our rooms. We had to shower and change quickly because Mrs. Bellaire was escorting us to the New York Philharmonic.

As soon as I was dressed, I started searching for Quinn's phone number. I rummaged through my suitcase, sure that I had left my wallet in an inside pocket, along with the keys to my dorm room. The keys were there, but no wallet. I fumbled through pants pockets and jackets, then I saw the wallet lying on the floor next to the suitcase. Usually I was more careful with it.

Quinn's number was tucked between his phone card and my driver's license. I pulled it out and started dialing.

"Hello, we're glad you called," a smooth male voice assured me. "Carville and Eaton are out on the slopes. Or—or, yes! We're partying down! If you want to join us, girls, please leave your name and number. . . ."

I tapped my fingers impatiently, waiting for the beep.

"Quinn? Me. I'm going to tell her."

Then I hung up. There was nothing else to say but the truth.

The symphony hall was filling up quickly with men and women in elegant clothes. Emily and Tracy had checked their long velvet capes. Mrs. Bellaire placed her mink on an empty seat at the end of our row.

It was Lonnie's seat. She had gone out with

the old boyfriend, and both Harper and Mrs. Bellaire were clearly annoyed, though for different reasons.

"You should have asked Lonnie long ago, Mum," Emily said as we sat down. "You can't expect her to be ready whenever we decide we want her to come along."

"After all I've done for that girl, I most certainly can expect a few things," Mrs. Bellaire replied.

"She's eighteen," Emily said quietly. "She has her own life now."

"She's ungrateful," said Mrs. Bellaire.

Harper looked miserable. Emily pressed her lips together silently and seemed relieved when her mother turned to chat with Dix. As usual, Mrs. Bellaire and Dix got along very well.

I sat next to Emily throughout the performance and kept glancing sideways. Her face was rapt with the music, washed with the soft light from the stage. Only her earrings moved, long and glittering against her neck. I longed to touch her and hoped that Emily would make the first move in front of her mother. But we did not even brush arms, much less hold hands during the performance.

I thought we'd have some time alone when we got home that evening. When I tried to get rid of Dix, however, Emily played the perfect hostess, suggesting we all go to the game room. I caught her eye a couple of times, but she glanced away quickly.

After the fourth game of Ping-Pong I got disgusted. "Well, good night," I said, throwing down my paddle.

"Are you tired?" Emily asked.

"I've had enough."

"Well . . . sleep tight," she said.

I might as well have slept on a bed of rocks. I tossed and turned and watched the clock till dawn, and when sleep finally came, it was no better. In one dream after another, I chased Emily through the Bellaire house. The lights were out and the air felt as cold as that half-frozen pond. Dix's face, attached to a spring like a jack-in-the-box, kept popping up between us, laughing.

I overslept, and by the time I arrived downstairs, breakfast had been cleared away. Mrs. Dove, dressed in her new plaid coat, met me in the kitchen.

"Oh, there you are, Quinn," she said. "You had a phone call early this morning, but I was reluctant to wake you up. It was from your friend Jeff."

I drew in my breath. "Did he leave a message?" I asked.

She bustled around the kitchen, pouring juice and putting muffins in the oven for me. "Yes, he said to tell you . . . " She hesitated. "These are his words, not mine, mind you: 'You're an idiot and a jerk.'"

"Okay."

"And he's counting on you to handle it so

190

that only Emily knows." Her voice was perfectly matter-of-fact. Her face did not betray any questions she might have about such a suspicious-sounding message.

"He'll be skiing this morning, so you won't be able to reach him," she added. "That's all."

"Thanks, Mrs. Dove. I can do the muffins," I told her. "It looks like you're on your way somewhere."

"Actually, I am, love. Thanks." She hurried up the back stairs.

I had just burned my hand on the oven when the kitchen door swung open. I muttered under my breath, then looked up. Emily.

"Good morning," she said. Her voice sounded uncertain about even that. She came halfway across the kitchen, then stopped, keeping a distance between us.

"Emily, we've got to talk."

"I know. I—I'm sorry about last night. Things are a little complicated right now." She took several steps closer, then came over and reached for my hand. "I guess you've figured out that Mum is impressed by Dix."

I stiffened.

"Don't be angry."

"Why not?" I asked.

"Because it doesn't help, okay? Give me some time to work things out."

Work things out? Emily's efforts would be useless once her mother found out who I was.

"It's hard for me," she began, her eyes begging me to understand.

"It's hard for me too." I took a deep breath. "Emily, there are things I have to tell you."

"Not now," she said quickly, letting go of my hand. "I can't talk now. Dovey and I are going out with Mum."

"When you come back, then."

She edged toward the door.

"We have to talk, Em. When you come back," I called after her, but she did not reply.

Sixteen

AT THREE-THIRTY IN the afternoon I stood at the window of the game room, watching for Emily's return. Outside the temperature was well above freezing; everything that had been snow-covered dripped, and a fog was settling in. Dix was with me, playing pool by himself, coolly calculating angles and sinking balls into pockets.

The car pulled up at three-forty-five. I rushed over to the main house and caught Emily halfway up the long stairs. My voice came out more sharply than I meant it to. "Emily!"

She spun around.

"Come down. Please," I said in a softer voice. "We have to talk. I'm not angry at you. It's me—I need to tell you a few things about me."

She came down the steps slowly, reluctantly.

I took both her hands in mine. "I don't know how to say this, but—"

"Emily! Quinn!" Lonnie came flying in from the dining room.

"Cripe, Lon, I'm—"

"Listen up," she said, cutting me short. "Harper just told me. Last night, before the concert, he and Dix talked to Mrs. Bellaire and got her to agree to a little surprise. Guess who's coming tonight to celebrate the end of the holidays—with their *son?*" she said to me.

"Tonight?" I choked.

Lonnie turned back to Emily. "Quinn's parents will be arriving at seven o'clock with the other houseguests."

I sat down on the steps. I should have seen it coming. Dix had been late getting to the barn the day before. I felt certain now that he had stayed back to snoop in my room and search my wallet.

I noticed that Emily seemed somewhat startled herself. But all she said was, "What a lovely surprise." She paused and then asked, "Where's Harper?"

"Changing his clothes for tea."

Emily started up the steps.

"Emily, I've got to talk to you!" I called to her.

"After tea," she said, and kept going.

"Lonnie, what am I going to do?" I whispered.

"Don't panic," she said. "We'll think of something. Right now I have to get tea. Act as if nothing is going on. Just be yourself—well, be Quinn, or whoever. We'll figure a way to get you out of here. Stay cool."

I stayed "cool" by going outside without a coat and pacing around in the fog. At five minutes after four, Lonnie found me and told me that I was expected in the library. Tea was being poured there that afternoon because the drawing room was being prepared for the New Year's celebration.

Mr. Bellaire sat in the corner, working on his papers. Mrs. Bellaire was showing the others the little favors that she and Emily had bought for their guests. I wondered which ones were for the Eatons. My palms and fingers were sweaty. Pansy kept licking them.

Dix had the same self-satisfied look that he'd worn the day before, but Harper refused to meet my eyes. Emily chatted with Tracy, wearing that polite dollface expression that made her look like her mother.

"I have to admit," Dix was saying, "I do miss my parents—but don't you dare tell them. I mean you, Tracy," he added, nudging his sister, and Mrs. Bellaire laughed pleasantly.

"How about you, Quinn?" he asked. "Have you missed your parents this holiday?"

"Yes."

"What traditions did you miss the most?" he asked.

"Just being with them."

"They're home now, aren't they?" Dix went on.

"Yes. They should be."

Mr. Bellaire glanced up from his corner, rubbing his chin thoughtfully.

"I'd like to meet them," Dix said, trying to get a reaction out of me.

"That would be great."

"Perhaps they could stop by tomorrow," Dix suggested, turning to Emily's mother. Behind Mrs. Bellaire's back, I saw Mr. Bellaire frown.

"I'd really like that," I lied. *Once I've told Emily, I'm out of here,* I thought.

"Warm shortbread?" Lonnie asked, unloading a tray.

"Perhaps you should give them a call," Dix persisted.

"Good idea!" I agreed.

Dix looked a little frustrated.

"Excuse me, madam," Robert said, entering the room. "The Eatons have arrived."

Lonnie's tray banged down on the table. I stared openmouthed at Mr. Dove.

Mrs. Bellaire laughed gaily and winked at Dix. "We were teasing you, Quinn," she said. "We had already invited them. Of course, we had no idea they'd arrive now. What perfect timing!"

Mr. Dove stepped aside and the Eatons entered.

"With the terrible fog," Mrs. Eaton began, bustling in, beaming at us all, "we decided to come early. I hope you don't mind."

"We're delighted," said Mrs. Bellaire.

"Aren't we, Quinn?" Dix asked in a clear voice. "Are you glad to see your parents?"

Mrs. Eaton squinted at me and took a few steps closer. She looked me over from head to toe, then glanced around the room, as if expecting to see her son hiding under a piece of furniture. Her smile faded. She turned to her husband, who was shaking hands with Mr. Bellaire. "Tyler," she called sharply.

"Right here, dear. Well, Quinn, have you had a—" He broke off.

"He's wearing Quinn's sweater," Mrs. Eaton said. "And Quinn's pants—I bought those pants. I didn't buy those shoes—his feet are too big."

"What are you talking about, Mandy?" Mrs. Bellaire asked.

"Interesting," said Mr. Bellaire, joining our group.

Emily's face was unreadable.

"Excuse me, madam," Mr. Dove broke in. "Another guest has just arrived for the festivities. Mr., uh . . . Mr. . . ." He shrugged, bowed politely, and stepped aside.

"Quinn!" Mrs. Eaton exclaimed, smiling again.

My roommate was wearing the exact same color sweater that I was and pants almost identical to the ones I had on. Our hair was cut by the same barber. Our shoes were similar, even if his feet were smaller. Everyone looked from him to me to him again.

"What the devil's going on?" Mr. Eaton asked.

"That is precisely what I'd like to know," said Mrs. Bellaire.

Mr. Bellaire grunted. "I wondered why I liked him."

"Emily, I'm sorry."

She turned to me, her eyes damp.

197

"It's all very easy to explain," Quinn said confidently.

This ought to be good, I thought.

"It was in late November—right, Jeff?" He was trying to drag me into his tale telling. I didn't respond.

"I accepted an invitation for the holidays from a school friend. A week later, I heard from my parents that I was invited to Deer Hill." Quinn's chronological order was just a *bit* off. "I didn't want to disappoint anyone and didn't know what to do. Then, not long after, my roommate—Jeff, here—got some bad news from home."

He looked at me as if expecting me to nod, confirming his story. I didn't move.

"Jeff goes to Maplecrest on scholarship and, as always, was trying to scrape together his airfare home to Arizona."

Well, now they all knew I had no money.

"His mother had to take care of a sick aunt, which left him with his father, who doesn't really have room for Jeff in his mobile home."

Mrs. Bellaire and Tracy looked shell-shocked.

"Interesting," said Mr. Bellaire.

Dix kept a poker face.

"I thought about it a bit," Quinn continued, "and I thought how well things would work out for everyone if I went with my friend and Jeff enjoyed the holidays at Deer Hill."

"Quinn always wants to please others," Mrs. Eaton said, smiling at her son.

"I called you and Dad early to wish you a happy New Year," Quinn told his mother. "That's when Mrs. Green informed me you had left for the Bellaires'. So I came right away—I didn't want *you* to be disappointed."

"Is any of this true?" Mr. Bellaire asked me.

"I faked it for Quinn, that's true," I said. "I lied about who I was—that's true too. What I did was wrong. I'm sorry, Emily, I really am."

She blinked but said nothing. Just looking at her made me hurt deep inside.

"Mr. and Mrs. Bellaire, I apologize. And Harper." I nodded at him.

His cheeks looked as red as mine felt. I didn't blame him for conspiring with Dix; he must have been really upset when he saw me with Lonnie.

"I am shocked," said Mrs. Bellaire. "Both Mr. Bellaire and I are unbelievably shocked."

"I'll go pack now," I said. "It won't take long. Can I get a taxi from here?"

"I'll take you in my car," Lonnie offered.

I wished Emily would say something.

"I'm coming along," Harper told us as Lonnie and I headed toward the hall.

She turned to him quickly and shook her head.

"Really, I'd like to," he said.

"I'm sorry, Harper. I'm dropping off Jeff, then going on to a friend's house."

"But it's New Year's Eve! You've always spent New Year's Eve with us," Harper insisted.

"This year I'm spending it with friends," she

said. "And I don't see what it matters to you."

He drew back, looking hurt.

"Tell her," I said. "Tell her, Harper, how much she matters."

He stared down at his hands.

"You know you've been in love with her for a long time," I went on. *Maybe one pair of us still has a chance,* I thought. "Don't make my mistake. Hiding your true feelings just screws everything up."

Lonnie stood still, her large eyes watchful, her hands over her mouth.

"Come on, Harper," I urged. "You know you can't stop thinking about her."

Harper stood mute as a statue.

"Well, I sure hope you guys figure it out." I sighed. "I'll be ready soon, Lon." I made a fast exit, nearly tripping over Pansy, who was waiting at the door. She followed me through the hall and drawing room, her tags jingling.

"You dumb dog." She kept following me. I finally leaned down to give her a quick pat. "Take care of Em for me. Chase away the jerks—just like you chased me. Maybe you're not so dumb." The dog looked up at me sweetly. I scratched her around the ears. "Stay close to her, pal, especially when she hurts." My throat was a lump. I straightened up quickly and headed for the guest wing.

"Jeff. Jeff!"

Just the sound of Emily saying my real name could make me stop breathing.

"Do you want to talk now?" she asked.

I turned toward her. "I think it's all been pretty well said."

Emily shook her head. "You haven't heard my side yet."

"Okay. Yell away."

"Who's Kate?"

She caught me off guard. "Kate?"

"Kate," she said firmly. "'I miss you,'" she said. "'Did you open your present? It'll look great on you. You're not clingy. I love you too.'"

Emily folded her arms, waiting for me to remember.

"You mean my mother, Kate?" I asked. "Were you the noise outside my room when I called her on Christmas?"

Emily leaned against the wall and closed her eyes. "Your mother. The one in the fringe. I can't believe it. Dix was in the hall, and he told me what he had overheard. He told me at Killington, after you got clobbered at lunch. It never occurred to me—your mother."

"You thought she was a girlfriend?" I started laughing. "How'd you know she was the one in the fringe?"

"She looks like you. In that photograph, she has the exact same expression as you do."

"But when I showed you the photo—"

Emily glanced away and smiled a little.

"Wait a minute," I said. "You suspected?"

"No." She met my eyes. "I knew."

"When did you know?" I demanded.

"Teatime, December twenty-third."

"What?"

"When you got that cup stuck on your finger. Lonnie and I conferred in the kitchen and came to the same conclusion."

"You—you were faking all this time!" I paced around the room. "And Lonnie knew you knew. You were both faking—"

"Now, just a minute," she said. "You started it. How do you think I felt when Quinn snubbed me and sent a guy in his place who couldn't handle china or stay on a horse? I mean, how stupid did you two think I was?"

"Uh . . ."

"How desperate?"

I shrugged helplessly.

"I said to myself, 'They want to play games? I'll play along.' And I played pretty well," Emily said proudly, "but I was afraid I had gone too far when I read you those romantic letters he was supposed to have written."

"Supposed. You made them up?"

"Of course. Quinn doesn't write in complete sentences."

I sat down, holding my head in my hands.

"As I told you before, I never expected to really fall for you," Emily said.

"I guess not."

"But I did," she added softly. "And I didn't know what to do about it."

I looked up. Her eyes were wet again.

"I've been feeling so mixed up and hurt. I figured as soon as you finished your job for Quinn, you'd fly off to Kate. In the end, the joke was on me."

I stood up. "On both of us, Em. I love you."

She put her arms around me and laid her head on my shoulder.

"I love you," I whispered softly. "But you know I can't stay at Deer Hill."

She didn't let go.

"Emily," I whispered, "you know I have to go." I could feel her tears against my neck. "I'm so sorry."

"I love you, love you," she said, holding on tightly. She kissed me. She pressed her mouth so tenderly against mine, I ached all over. I closed my eyes and clung to her.

When I opened them again, I noticed that the drawing room doors had been closed and Pansy was not in sight.

"Okay," Emily said, taking a deep breath. "Okay! Time to tell them. You're staying here, or I'm going. And when we go back to school, I'm writing you letters that will make you blush to your toes, Jeff. Will you come with me while I tell them?"

"Could you leave out that part about the letters?"

She laughed and opened the heavy door. "Dad!" she said, surprised.

Her father was sitting on the center hall steps, tapping his foot.

"Is something wrong?" she asked.

"You be the judge, Emily," Mr. Bellaire replied. "You heard what was said in the other room. Now your mother has retired to her bedroom with a migraine."

"I'm sorry," Emily said contritely.

"That, of course, makes me tonight's host," he added, "which ought to make it a miserable affair."

Emily nodded in agreement.

"I thought you should know, in case you prefer to go with Lonnie and Harper to another party."

"You mean Lonnie and Harper will be going together?" Emily asked.

"Pasted to each other, it appears."

Emily smiled and put her arm around me. "I— I'd like to stay here and celebrate with you, Dad. If Jeff can."

Mr. Bellaire looked at me and pulled himself up. "I suppose you'll want to kiss her at midnight."

"Yes, sir."

"Well, you'll have to do it before or after," he said, "because I'll need a hand. I've decided to end this ridiculous affair by ringing in the New Year with the original Bell-ringer Special bell."

"Don't you think that's a little tacky, Dad?" Emily asked.

"Of course it is," Mr. Bellaire replied, and strode away, chuckling to himself.

"Whew!" said Emily.

I beckoned to her, and she joined me at the long window next to the front door. Through the glass we could see Harper walking with his arm around Lonnie, his head bent close to hers.

With twilight falling, the lighted tree in the hall and our own faces—mine above Emily's—were reflected in the same glass.

"Look at them, Jeff," she said.

"Look at us," I replied softly.

Are You Changing Yourself for Your Guy?

So you've found your true love, and life is bliss. You two have so much in common—you share the same tastes, love the same bands . . . or do you? Sometimes opposites attract, and maybe your guy has a totally different style. The big question is, are you still the same person you were before you met him? Or are you becoming his clone? Take Jenny and Jake's love quiz to see if you're changing too much for your boyfriend.

1. You hate Metallica, but he loves them and they're having a concert in your area. You:

  A. Tell him to go and have a good time with his friends, and you'll see him later.

  B. Buy the CD and really try to see what he loves about the music, but when the appeal still eludes you, skip the concert.

  C. Snag tickets for the best seats you can get and headbang right along with him.

2. You and your best friend have a standing date for Friday night dinners, but your guy insists that you should be spending Friday nights with him. You decide to:

A. Continue to have dinner with your friend every week. He'll have to understand that this is the way things are.
B. Ask your friend if you can change the night you spend together.
C. Explain to your friend that you have to spend as much time with your boyfriend as he wants, and you'll still try to have dinner with her once in a while.

3. He signed up for classes that really don't interest you. You haven't chosen your classes yet. What do you do?

A. Decide that it's more important to be around him than to take the courses you really like, and arrange your schedule to match his.
B. Sign up for the kinds of classes you usually take. After all, you can still hang out together after school.
C. Shakespeare may be more fun than you thought. You'll give that one a try but you'll pick the rest yourself.

4. You have always loved your long hair, but he says girls with short hair are really sexy. The next time you're at the hairdresser you say:

A. Chop it off!
B. My usual trim, please.
C. I think I'll try something new, but not too short.

5. When you hang out with your friends they:

A. Act the same as they always have.
B. Seem a little uncomfortable.
C. Tell you they miss your company, but they're glad things are the same when you are around.

6. He uses the word rad *all the time*. You find yourself:

A. Teasing him about his outdated word choice.
B. Adding the word to your vocabulary—along with other rad terms he uses.
C. Accidentally using the word once or twice, and then laughing at yourself.

7. He tells you he thinks teen magazines are stupid. Your response:

A. You promptly throw out your whole treasured collection of *YM*.
B. You agree that he might be right, but hold on to the magazines anyway.
C. You buy the next month's issue of *Seventeen* and tell him that *Beavis and Butt-head* isn't exactly enlightened either.

8. You need eight hours of sleep to function, but he can't talk on the phone until late at night. Your new average sleep time per night is:

A. Still eight hours—you keep the weeknight phone conversations short.

B. Let's just say caffeine is your only hope of making it through the day.

C. It depends on the night; sometimes you'll stay up late talking, and other nights you'll get to bed at your regular time.

9. *You like short skirts, but he thinks you should dress conservatively. You:*

A. Wear only the clothing that he likes to see you in.

B. Continue to wear short skirts, but only when you know you won't see him.

C. Tell him that you appreciate his advice but you'll wear whatever you choose.

10. *How often do you pretend to love something he loves?*

A. Rarely. You did it more when you first met, but now you usually tell him how you really feel.

B. Never—why should you ever need to?

C. All the time—that's what being in love means.

11. *You love fancy restaurants, but McDonald's is more his style. When you go out to dinner you:*

A. Take turns choosing where to go.

B. Always end up at a fast-food place. In fact, the food there is growing on you.

C. Refuse to let him take you to anywhere you don't want to eat.

12. He takes up in-line skating. You've never had the greatest sense of balance. You:

A. Watch him from the sidewalk.
B. Rush out to buy in-line skates along with all the protective gear.
C. Try it once or twice, but quit when you get tired of falling on your butt.

SCORING:

1)	a=1	b=2	c=3
2)	a=1	b=2	c=3
3)	a=3	b=1	c=2
4)	a=3	b=1	c=2
5)	a=1	b=3	c=2
6)	a=1	b=3	c=2
7)	a=3	b=2	c=1
8)	a=1	b=3	c=2
9)	a=3	b=2	c=1
10)	a=2	b=1	c=3
11)	a=2	b=3	c=1
12)	a=1	b=3	c=2

12–19:

You're a true independent! You know that boys come and go, and you don't think your identity should come and go with them. Congrats for holding true to who you are, but just be careful that you're not a little too stubborn. After all, sometimes you can learn a lot from trying new things, and your guy might introduce you to something you really love.

20–27:

You know who you are, but you're also willing to bend a little to make him happy. You still remember how important your friends are, and you wouldn't let him take over your life. As long as you make sure that you hold your ground for what really matters to you, then it's fine to compromise.

28–36:

Okay, now when was the last time you made a decision on your own? If you're changing everything about yourself for this guy, it's time to stop and think. A little change is healthy, but if you give yourself a total makeover, then you aren't even the girl he asked out in the first place! Guys want girls who are confident, and in the long run you'll only be happy if you know he likes you for who you really are.

Do you ever wonder about falling in love? About members of the opposite sex? Do you need a little friendly advice but have no one to turn to? Well, that's where we come in . . . Jenny and Jake. Send us those questions you're dying to ask, and we'll give you the straight scoop on life and love in the nineties.

DEAR JAKE

Q: *After my ex-boyfriend and I broke up, we stayed good friends. The problem now is that I still love him and I want to tell him. If I do, will it scare him away?*

AL North Adams, MA

A: Are you kidding? We men aren't scared of anything! Except, of course, of girls who tell us they love us. Here's the deal: It's possible that your ex still feels the same way about you, and you guys want the same thing. But it's also possible that you broke up for a reason and he's happy the way things are.

Before you bare your soul to him and risk the friendship that you have, try to watch for clues about how he feels. Is he dating anyone else yet? Does he talk to you about other girls? A yes to these questions should make you pause. On the other hand, does he still spend important nights hanging out with you, or seem jealous when you talk about other guys? If all these signs point to a green light, then try to ask him casually how he would feel about dating again. Then, when he tells you he's all for it, go ahead and let him know how you feel. Good luck!

DEAR JENNY

Q: *My friend Lena has a crush on this guy, and she's going out on a date with him this weekend. I'm worried about her because he has another girlfriend and she knows it. I don't want to see her become the other woman. Is there anything I can do to stop her from getting hurt?*

RM Pittsburgh, PA

A: They say that there are always obstacles to every great romance. However, the fact that this guy has a girlfriend is an obstacle Lena will have real problems overcoming. Yes, it's possible they have something special and he'll realize it and break up with his girlfriend. The two of them will then have a glorious love that will last for ages.

The real truth? If he'll do it to this girlfriend, he'll do it to Lena. Besides, what if he never leaves the girlfriend and just keeps stringing both girls along? You're right to worry about your friend; nothing good can come of this. Tell her you're concerned, and that she deserves a guy who will love her and only her. But unfortunately, when it comes down to it, she's going to make her own choices. Let her know you're there for her, and be ready to pick up the pieces when he breaks her heart.

Do you have questions about love? Write to:

Jenny Burgess or Jake Korman
c/o Daniel Weiss Associates
33 West 17th Street
New York, NY 10011